Mrs Audrey

True Tales of Mountain Adventures For Non-Climbers Young and Old

Mrs Audrey Le Blond

True Tales of Mountain Adventures For Non-Climbers Young and Old

1st Edition | ISBN: 978-3-75240-906-2

Place of Publication: Frankfurt am Main, Germany

Year of Publication: 2020

Outlook Verlag GmbH, Germany.

Reproduction of the original.

TRUE TALES OF MOUNTAIN ADVENTURE

Melchior Anderegg 1894.
BY
MRS AUBREY LE BLOND

PREFACE

There is no manlier sport in the world than mountaineering.

It is true that all the sports Englishmen take part in are manly, but mountaineering is different from others, because it is sport purely for the sake of sport. There is no question of beating any one else, as in a race or a game, or of killing an animal or a bird as in hunting or shooting. A mountaineer sets his skill and his strength against the difficulty of getting to the top of a steep peak. Either he conquers the mountain, or it conquers him. If he fails, he keeps on trying till he succeeds. This teaches him perseverance, and proves to him that anything is possible if he is determined to do it.

In mountaineering, all the party share the pleasures and the dangers. Every climber has to help the others. Every climber has to rely both on himself and on his companions.

Mountaineering makes a person quick in learning how to act in moments of danger. It cultivates his presence of mind, it teaches him to be unselfish and thoughtful for others who may be with him. It takes him amongst the grandest scenery in the world, it shows him the forces of nature let loose in the blinding snow-storm, or the roaring avalanche. It lifts him above all the petty friction of daily life, and takes him where the atmosphere is always pure, and the outlook calm and wide. It brings him health, and leaves him delightful recollections. It gives him friends both amongst his fellow-climbers, and in the faithful guides who season after season accompany him. It is a pursuit which he can commence early in life, and continue till old age, for the choice of expeditions is endless, and ascents of all scales of difficulty and of any length are easily found.

That I do not exaggerate the joys and the benefits of mountaineering will be borne out by those extracts from the true tales from the hills of which this book chiefly consists. Some may think I have dwelt at undue length on the catastrophes which have darkened the pages of Alpine history. I do not apologize. If in one single instance any one who reads these pages becomes afterwards a climber, and takes warning from anything I have told him, I am amply justified.

It has been difficult in a work like this to know always what to include and what to omit. My guiding principle has been to give preference to descriptions which are either so exciting by reason of the facts narrated, or else so brilliantly and wittily written, that they cannot fail to excite the reader's interest. To these I have added four chapters, those on mountaineering, on glaciers, on avalanches, and on the guides of the Alps, which may help to make climbing more intelligible to those who have never attempted it.

My warm thanks are due to Sir Leslie Stephen, Messrs Whymper, Tuckett, Charles Pilkington, and Clinton Dent who have rendered the production of this book possible by allowing me to quote at considerable length from their writings; also to Messrs Longman who have permitted me to make extracts from works of which they hold the copyright, and to Messrs Newnes and Messrs Hutchinson for their kind permission to re-print portions of my articles which have appeared in their publications.

I am also under a debt of gratitude to Mr Philip Gosset, who has not only allowed me to reprint his account of the avalanche on the Haut-de-Cry, but has also most kindly placed his wide knowledge of glaciers at my disposal by offering to revise the chapter I have written on that subject in this book.

Dr Kennedy, whose beautiful edition of Mr Moore's diary, "The Alps in 1864," recently appeared, has generously given me permission to make any extracts I desire from it.

Colonel Arkwright, whose brother perished on Mont Blanc in 1866, has been good enough to allow me to reproduce a most interesting and hitherto unpublished photograph of the relics discovered in 1897.

The illustrations, except those connected with the Arkwright accident, and a view of the Matterhorn, by the late Mr W. F. Donkin, are from photographs by me. By them I have tried rather to show how climbers carry out their mountaineering than to illustrate any particular locality.

In my own writings I have adopted, in the spelling of names of places, the modern official forms, but, of course, when quoting I have kept to those followed by each writer.

If, in the following pages, I have given any pleasure to those who have never scaled a peak, or have perhaps recalled happy days amongst the mountains to a fellow-climber, it will be a very real gratification to me.

E. LE BLOND.

67, THE DRIVE,
BRIGHTON, *Oct. 30th, 1902.*

CHAPTER I

WHAT IS MOUNTAINEERING?

Mountaineering is not merely walking up hill. It is the art of getting safely up and down a peak where there is no path, and where steps may have to be cut in the ice; it is the art of selecting the best line of ascent under conditions which vary from day to day.

Mountaineering as a science took long to perfect. It is more than a century since the first ascent of a big Alpine peak was accomplished, and the early climbers had but little idea of the dangers which they were likely to meet with. They could not tell when the snow was safe, or when it might slip away in an avalanche. They did not know where stones would be likely to fall on them, or when they were walking over one of those huge cracks in the glacier known as crevasses, and lightly bridged over with winter snow, which might break away when they trod on it. However, they soon learnt that it was safer for two or more people to be together in such places than for a man to go alone, and when crossing glaciers they used the long sticks they carried as a sort of hand-rail, a man holding on to each end, so that if one tumbled into a hole the other could pull him out. Of course this was a very clumsy way of doing things, and before long it occurred to them that a much better plan would be to use a rope, and being all tied to it about 20 feet apart, their hands were left free, and the party could go across a snow-field and venture on bridged-over crevasses in safety.

At first both guides and travellers carried long sticks called alpenstocks. If they came to a steep slope of hard snow or ice, they hacked steps up it with small axes which they carried slung on their backs. This was a very inconvenient way of going to work, as it entailed holding the alpenstock in one hand and using the axe with the other. So they thought of a better plan, and had the alpenstock made thicker and shorter, and fastened an axe-head to the top of it. This was gradually improved till it became the ice-axe, as used to-day, and as shown in many of my photographs. This ice-axe is useful for various purposes besides cutting steps. If you dig in the head while crossing a snow-slope, it acts as an anchor, and gives tremendous hold, while to allude to its functions as a tin-opener, a weapon of defence against irate bulls on Alpine pastures, or as a means for rapidly passing through a crowd at a railway station, is but to touch on a very few of its admirable qualities.

CLIMBERS DESCENDING A SNOW-CLAD PEAK (THE ORTLER).

When people first climbed they went in droves on the mountains, or I should say rather on the mountain, for during the first half of the nineteenth century Mont Blanc was the object of nearly all the expeditions which set out for the eternal snows. After some years, however, it was found quite unnecessary to have so many guides and porters, and nowadays a party usually numbers four, two travellers and two guides, or three, consisting generally of one traveller and two guides, or occasionally five. Two is a bad number, as should one of them be hurt or taken ill, the other would have to leave him and go for help, though one of the first rules of mountaineering is that a man who is injured or indisposed must never be left alone on a mountain. Again, six is not a good number; it is too many, as the members of the party are sure to get in each other's way, pepper each other with stones, and waste no end of time in wrangling as to when to stop for food, when to proceed, and which way to go up. A good guide will run the concern himself, and turn a deaf ear to all suggestions; but the fact remains that six people had better split up and go on separate ropes. And if they also, in the case of rock peaks, choose different mountains, it is an excellent plan. The best of friends are apt to revile each other when stones, upset from above, come whistling about their ears.

The early mountaineers were horribly afraid of places which were at all difficult to climb. Mere danger, however, had no terrors for them, and they calmly encamped on frail snow-bridges, or had lunch in the path of avalanches. After a time the dangerous was understood and avoided, and the difficult grappled with by increased skill, until about the middle of the nineteenth century there arose a class of experts, little, if at all, inferior to the best guides of the present day.

The most active and intelligent of the natives of Chamonix, Zermatt, and the Bernese Oberland now learnt to find their way even on mountains new to them. Some were chamois hunters, and accustomed to climb in difficult places. Others, perhaps, had when boys minded the goats, and scrambled after them in all sorts of awkward spots. Others, again, had such a taste for mountaineering that they took to it the very first time they tried it. Of these last my own guide, Joseph Imboden, was one, and later on I will tell you of the extraordinary way in which he began his splendid career.

ON A ROCK RIDGE NEAR THE TOP OF MONTE ROSA.

The Schallihorn may be seen in the top right-hand corner of the picture.

It is from going with and watching how good guides climb that most people learn to become mountaineers themselves. Nearly all take guides whenever they ascend difficult mountains, but some are so skilful and experienced that they go without, though few are ever good enough to do this quite safely.

I am often asked why people climb, and it is a hard question to answer satisfactorily. There is something which makes one long to mountaineer more and more, from the first time one tries it. All climbs are different. All views from mountains are different, and every time one climbs one is uncertain, owing to the weather or the possible state of the peak, if the top can be reached or not. So it is always a struggle between the mountain and the climber, and though perseverance, skill, experience, and pluck must give the victory to the climber in the end, yet the fight may be a long one, and it may be years before a particularly awkward peak allows one to stand on its summit.

Perhaps, if you have patience to read what follows, you may better understand what mountaineering is, and why most of those who have once tried it become so fond of it.

THE ALETSCH GLACIER FROM BEL ALP.

The medial moraine is very conspicuous. This glacier is about a mile in width.

CHAPTER II

A FEW WORDS ABOUT GLACIERS

Of all the beautiful and interesting things mountain districts have to show, none surpass the glaciers.

Now a glacier is simply a river of ice, which never melts away even during the hottest summer. Glaciers form high up on mountains, where there is a great deal of snow in winter, and where it is never very hot even in summer. They are also found in northern lands, such as Greenland, and there, owing to the long cold winter and short summer, they come down to the very level of the sea.

A glacier is formed in this way: There is a heavy fall of snow which lies in basins and little valleys high up on the mountain side. The air is too cold for it to melt, and as more falls on the top of it the mass gets pressed down. Now, if you take a lump of snow in your hand and press it, you get an icy snow-ball. If you squeeze anything you make it warmer. The pressing down of the great mass of snow is like the squeezing of the ball in your hand. It makes it warmer, so that the snow first half melts and then gradually becomes ice. You bring about this change in your snow-ball in a moment. Nature, in making a glacier, takes much longer, so that what was snow one year is only partly ice the next—it is known as *nevé*—and it is not until after several seasons that it becomes the pure ice we see in the lower part of a glacier.

One would fancy that if a quantity of snow falls every winter and does not all melt, the mountains must grow higher. But though only a little of the snow melts, it disappears in other ways. Some is evaporated into the atmosphere; some falls off in avalanches. Most of it slowly flows down after forming itself into glaciers. For glaciers are always moving. The force of gravity makes them slide down over their rocky beds. They flow so slowly that we cannot see them move, in fact most of them advance only a few inches a day. But if a line of stakes is driven into the ice straight across a glacier, we shall notice in a few weeks that they have moved down. And the most interesting part of it is that they will not have moved evenly, but those nearest the centre will have advanced further than those at the side. In short, a glacier flows like a river, the banks keeping back the ice at the side, as the banks of a river prevent it from running so fast at the edge as in the middle.

General View on the Lower Part of a Large Glacier.

The surface is ice, not snow. The snow-line may be seen further up.

A large glacier is fed by such a gigantic mass of snow that it is in its upper part hundreds of feet thick. Of course when it reaches warmer places it begins to melt. But the quantity of ice composing it is so great that it takes a long time before it disappears, and a big glacier sometimes flows down far below the wild and rocky parts of mountains and reaches the neighbourhood of forests and corn-fields. It is very beautiful at Chamonix to see the white, glittering ice of the Glacier des Bossons flowing in a silent stream through green meadows.

The reason that mountaineers have to be careful in crossing glaciers is on account of the holes, cracks, or, to call them by their proper name, crevasses, which are met with on them. Ice, unlike water, is brittle, so it splits up into crevasses whenever the glacier flows over a steep or uneven rocky bed. High up, where snow still lies, these chasms in the ice are often bridged over, and if a person ventures on one of these snow bridges it may break, and he may fall down the crevasse, which may be so deep that no bottom can be found to it. He is then either killed by the fall or frozen to death. If, as I have explained before, several climbers are roped together, they form a long string, like the tail of a kite, and not more than one is likely to break through at a time. As the rope is—or ought to be—kept tightly stretched, he cannot fall far, and is easily pulled out again.

The snow melts away off the surface of the glacier further down in summer. It is on this bare, icy stream, scarred all over with little channels full of water running merrily down the melting rough surface, that the ordinary tourist is taken when he visits a glacier during his summer trip to Switzerland.

A GLACIER TABLE (page 11).

Taken in Mid-Winter on reaching the Lower Slopes of a Mountain after a terrific Storm of Snow and Wind. The local Swiss snow-shoes were used during part of the ascent.

You will notice in most of the photographs of glaciers black streaks along them, sometimes only near the sides, sometimes also in the centre. These are heaps of stones and earth which have fallen from the mountains bordering the glacier, and have been carried along by the slowly moving ice. The bands in the centre have come there, owing to the meeting higher up of two glaciers, which have joined their side heaps of rubbish, and have henceforward flowed on as one glacier. The bands of piled up stones are called moraines, those at the edge being known as lateral moraines, in the centre as medial moraines, and the stones which drop off the end (or snout) of a glacier, as terminal moraines.

Besides these compact bands, we sometimes find here and there a big stone or boulder by itself, which has rolled on to the ice. Often these stones are raised on a pedestal of ice, and then they are called "glacier-tables." They have covered the bit of ice they lie upon, and prevented it from melting, while the glacier all round has gradually sunk. After a time the leg of the table begins to feel the sun strike it also. It melts away on the south side and the stone slips off. A party of climbers, wandering about on a glacier at night or in a fog, and having no compass, can roughly take their bearings by noticing in what position these broken-down glacier-tables lie.

Occasionally sand has been washed down over the surface of the ice, and a patch of it has collected in one place. This shields the glacier from the sun, the surrounding ice sinks, and eventually we find cones which are lightly covered with sand, the smooth ice beneath being reached directly we scratch the surface with the point of a stick.

It is difficult to realise the enormous size of a large glacier. The Aletsch Glacier, the most extensive in the Alps, would, it has been said, if turned to stone, supply building material for a city the size of London.

With regard to the movement of glaciers, the entertaining author of "A Tramp Abroad" mildly chaffs his readers by telling them that he once tried to turn a glacier to account as a means of transport. Accordingly, he took up his position in the middle, where the ice moves quickest, leaving his luggage at the edge, where it goes slowest. Thus he intended to travel by express, leaving his things to follow by goods train! However, after some time, he appeared to make no progress, so he got out a book on glaciers to try and find out the reason for the delay. He was much surprised when he read that a glacier moves at about the same pace as *the hour hand of a watch*!

A DISTORTED AND CREVASSED GLACIER.

Showing the rough texture of the surface of a Glacier below the Snow-line.

Many thousands of years ago there were glaciers in Scotland and England.

We are certain of this, as glaciers scratch and polish the rocks they pass over as does nothing else. Stones are frozen into the ice, and it holds them and uses them as we might hold and use a sharply-pointed instrument, scratching the rock over which the mighty mass is slowly passing. In addition to the scratches, the ice polishes the rock till it is quite smooth, writing upon it in characters never to be effaced the history of past events. Another thing which proves to us that these icy rivers were in many places where there are no glaciers now, is the boulders we find scattered about. These boulders are sometimes of a kind of rock not found anywhere near, and so we know that they must have been carried along on that wonderful natural luggage-train, and dropped off it as it melted. We find big stones in North Wales which must have come on a glacier beginning in Scotland! Glacier-polished rocks are found along the whole of the west coast of Norway, and there are boulders near Geneva, in Switzerland, which have come from the chain of Mount Blanc, 60 miles away.

So you see that the glaciers of the Alps are far smaller than they were at one time, and that in many places where formerly there were huge glaciers, there are to-day none. The Ice Age was the time when these great glaciers existed, but the subject of the Ice Age is a difficult and thorny one, which is outside the scope of my information and of this book.

CHAPTER III

AVALANCHES

Many of the most terrible accidents in the Alps have been due to avalanches, and perhaps, as avalanches take place from different causes and have various characteristics, according to whether they are of ice, snow, or *débris*, some account of them may not be out of place.

We may briefly classify them as follows:—

1. Ice avalanches, only met with on or near glaciers.
2. Dust avalanches, composed of very light, powdery snow.
3. Compact avalanches (*Grund* or ground avalanches, as the Germans call them), consisting of snow, earth, stones, trees, and anything which the avalanche finds in its path. These take place only in winter and spring, while the two other kinds happen on the mountains at any season.

An ice avalanche is easily understood when it is borne in mind that a glacier is always moving. When this river of ice comes to the edge of a precipice, or tries to crawl down a very steep cliff, it splits across and forms tottering crags of ice, which lean over more and more till they lose their balance and go crashing down the slope. Some of the ice is crushed to powder by its fall, yet many blocks generally survive, and are occasionally heaped up in such huge masses below that they form another glacier on a small scale. If a party of mountaineers passes under a place overhung by threatening ice, they are in great danger, though at early morning, before the sun has loosened the frozen masses, the peril is less. Sometimes, too, if the distance to be traversed is very short and the going quite easy, it is safe enough to dash quickly across.

**A TUNNEL 300 FEET LONG THROUGH AN AVALANCHE.
Tree trunks, etc., can be seen embedded in it.**

AN AVALANCHE NEAR BOUVERET, LAKE OF GENEVA.
Dust avalanches occur when a heavy fall of light, powdery snow takes place

on frozen hillsides or ice-slopes, and so long as there is no wind or disturbance, all remains quiet, and inexperienced people would think there was no danger. But in reality dust avalanches are the most to be feared of any, for they fall irregularly in unexpected places, and their power is tremendous. While all seems calm and peaceful, suddenly a puff of wind or the passage of an animal disturbs the delicately-balanced masses, and then woe betide whoever is within reach of this frightful engine of destruction. First, the snow begins to slide gently down, then it gathers pace and volume, and even miles away the thunder of its fall can be heard as it leaps from ledge to ledge. Covered with a cloud of smoking, powdery dust, it is a veritable Niagara of giant height, and as it descends towards the forests, it carries with it whatever it finds in its path. Trees are mown down with as much ease as the tender grass of spring. Houses are lifted from the ground and tossed faraway.

An avalanche is preceded by a blast even more destructive than the masses of snow which it hurls along. As it advances with ever-increasing rapidity the air in front is more and more compressed as the avalanche rushes on with lightning-like speed behind it. The wind sweeps everything before it, and many are the tales related by those who have survived or witnessed a display of its power. On one occasion more than a hundred houses were overwhelmed by a huge avalanche at Saas (Prättigau, near Davos), and during the search afterwards the rescue party found amidst the ruins a child lying asleep and uninjured in his cradle, which had been blown to some distance from his home, while close by stood a basket containing six eggs, none of which were broken. I have myself seen a row of telegraph posts in an Alpine valley in winter thrown flat on the ground by the air preceding an enormous avalanche, which itself did not come within 300 yards of them. It is a very wonderful thing that persons buried beneath an avalanche can sometimes hear every word spoken by a search party, and yet not a sound that they utter reaches the ears of those outside. A great deal of air is imprisoned between the particles of snow, and so it is possible for those overwhelmed by an avalanche to live inside it for hours. Cases have been known where a man, buried not far below the surface, has been able to melt a hole to the outer air with his breath, and eventually free himself from his icy prison. On 18th January, 1885, enormous avalanches fell in some of the mountainous districts of northern Italy, houses, cattle, crops, and granaries being carried away, and many victims buried beneath the ruins. Some touching episodes of wonderful escapes were related. "For instance, at Riva, in the valley of Susa, a whole family, consisting of an old woman of seventy, her two daughters, her four nieces, and a child four months old, were buried with their house in the snow, exposed apparently to certain death from cold and hunger. But the soldiers of the Compagnie Alpine, hearing of the sad case, worked with all their might and main to save them, and at last they were found and brought out alive, the brave old grandmother insisting that the children should be saved first, and then her daughters, saying that their lives were more precious than her own." The soldiers, who worked with a will above all praise, were obliged in several cases to construct long galleries in the snow in order to reach the villages, which were sometimes buried beneath 40 feet of snow.

Compact avalanches, though very terrible on account of their frequently great size, can be more easily guarded against than dust avalanches, because they always fall in well-defined channels. A compact avalanche consists of snow, earth, stones, and trees, and comes down in times of thaw. Many fall in early spring in Alpine valleys, and though it is not unusual for them to come right across high roads, the fatal accidents are comparatively few. The inhabitants know that wherever, high up on the hills, there is a hollow which may serve as a *reservoir* or collecting-basin for the snow, and below this a funnel or shoot, there an avalanche may be expected. Often they take means to prevent one starting, for an avalanche, whose power is irresistible when once it has begun to move quickly, is very easily kept from mischief if it is not allowed a running start. The best of all ways for preventing avalanches is to plant the gullies with trees, but where this cannot be done, rows of stakes driven into the ground will serve to hold up the snow, and where the hillside is extremely steep, and much damage would be caused if an avalanche fell, stone walls are built one above another to keep the soil and the snow together, very much as we see on precipitous banks overlooking English railways.

The driving roads over Alpine passes are in places exposed to avalanches in winter. At the worst spots galleries of stone are built, through which the sleighs can pass in perfect safety, and if an avalanche fell while they were inside it would pass harmlessly over their heads. On the Albula Pass, in Switzerland, as soon as the avalanches come down, tunnels are cut in the snow through them, and are in constant use till early summer.

Occasionally houses or churches are built in the very path of an avalanche. A V-shaped wall, called an avalanche-breaker, is put behind, and this cuts the snowy stream in two parts, which passes on harmlessly on either side of the building. Sometimes avalanche-breakers of snow, hardened into ice by throwing water over them, are constructed behind barns which have been put in exposed places.

In order that an avalanche may get up speed enough to commence its swift career, the slope the snow rests on where it starts must be at an angle of from 30° to 35° at least.

CHAPTER IV

THE GUIDES OF THE ALPS: WHAT THEY ARE AND WHAT THEY DO

There is no profession drawing its members from the peasant class which requires a combination of so many high and rare qualities as that of a mountain guide. Happily, the dwellers in hill countries seem usually more noble in mind and robust of frame than the inhabitants of plains, and all who know them well must admit that among Alpine guides are to be found men whose intelligence and character would rank high in any class of life.

I have usually noticed that the abilities and duties of a guide are little understood by the non-climber, who often imagines that a guide's sole business is to know the way and to carry the various useless articles which the beginner in mountaineering insists on taking with him.

EDOUARD CUPELIN OF CHAMONIX.

The Guide with whom Mrs Aubrey Le Blond commenced her climbing.

Guiding, if it sometimes does include these duties, is far more than this. The first-class guide must be the general of the little army setting out to invade the higher regions. He need not *know* the way—in fact, it sometimes happens that he has never before visited the district—but he must be able to *find* a way, and a safe one, to the summit of the peak for which his party is bound. An inferior guide may know, from habit, the usual way up a mountain, but, should the conditions of ice and snow alter, he is unable to alter with them and vary his route. You may ask: "How does a guide find his way on a mountain new to him?" There are several means open to him. If the peak is well known, as is, say, the Matterhorn, he will have heard from other guides which routes have been followed, and will know that if he desires to take his traveller up the ordinary way he must go past the Schwarz-see Hotel, and on to the ridge which terminates in the Hörnli, making for the hut which he has seen from below through the telescope. Then he remembers that he must cross to the east face, and while doing so he will notice the scratches on the rocks from the nailed boots of previous climbers. Now, mounting directly upward, he will pick out the passages which seem easiest, until, passing the ruined upper hut, he comes out on the ridge and looks down the tremendous precipice which overhangs the Matterhorn Glacier. This ridge, he knows, he simply has to follow until he reaches the foot of a steep face of rock some 50 feet high, down which hangs a chain. He has heard all about this bit of the climb since his boyhood, and he tells his traveller that, once on the top of the rock, all difficulty will be over, and the final slope to the summit will be found a gentle one. So it comes to pass that the party reaches the highest pinnacle of the great mountain without once diverging from the best route. Occasionally the leading guide may take with him as second guide a man from the locality, but most climbers will prefer to keep with them the two guides they are used to.

It is not only on mountains that a guide is able to find his way over little known ground. Many years ago Melchior Anderegg came to stay with friends in England, and arrived at London Bridge Station in the midst of a thick London fog. "He was met by Mr Stephen and Mr Hinchliff," writes his biographer in *The Pioneer of the Alps*, "who accompanied him on foot to the rooms of the latter gentleman in Lincoln's Inn Fields. A day or two later the same party found themselves at the same station on their return from Woolwich. 'Now, Melchior,' said Mr Hinchliff, 'you will lead us back home.' Instantly the skilful guide, who had never seen a larger town than Berne, accepted the situation, and found his way straight back without difficulty, pausing for consideration only once, as if to examine the landmarks at the foot of Chancery Lane."

Now, let us see how a guide sets about exploring a district where no one has previously ascended the mountains. Of this work I have seen a good deal, since in Arctic Norway my Swiss guides and I have ascended more than twenty hitherto-unclimbed peaks, and were never once unable to reach the summit. Of course, the first thing is to see the mountains, and, to do this, it is wise to ascend something which you are sure, from its appearance, is easy, and then prospect for others, inspecting others again from them, and so on, *ad infinitum*. You cannot always see the whole of a route, and, perhaps, your leading guide will observe: "We can reach that upper glacier by the gully in the rocks." "What gully?" you ask. "The one to the left. There *must* be one there. Look at the heap of stones at the bottom!" Thus, from the seen to the unseen the guide argues, reading a fact from writing invisible to the untrained eye. Between difficulty and danger, too, he draws a sharp distinction, and attacks with full confidence a steep but firm wall of rock, turning back from the easy-looking slope of snow ready to set forth in an avalanche directly the foot touches it.

And how is this proficiency obtained? How does the guide learn his profession?

In different ways, but he usually begins young, tending goats on steep grassy slopes requiring balance and nerve to move about over. Later on, having decided that he wishes to be a guide, the boy, at the age of seventeen or eighteen, offers himself for examination on applying for a certificate as porter. The requirements for this first step are not great: a good character, a sound physique, a knowledge of reading and writing, and in most Alpine centres the guild of guides will grant him a license. He can now accompany any guide who will take him, on any expedition that guide considers within the porter's powers. His advancement depends on his capacity. Should he quickly adapt himself to the work, the guides will trust him more and more, taking him on difficult ascents and allowing him occasionally to share the responsibility of leading on an ascent and coming down last when descending. It will readily be seen that the leader must never slip, and must, when those who follow are moving, be able to hold them should anything go wrong with them. The same applies to the even more responsible position of last man coming down. When a porter reaches this stage, he is little inferior to a second guide. He can now enter for his final examination. If he is competent, he has no trouble in passing it, and I fear that if the contrary—as is the case in many of those who apply—he gets through easily enough.

At Chamonix the guides' society is controlled by Government. The rules press hardly on the better class of guides there, or would do so if observed; but a first-class guide is practically independent of them, and mountaineers who know the ropes can avoid the regulations. At Zermatt greater liberty is allowed, and, indeed, I believe that everywhere except at Chamonix a guide is free to go with any climber who applies for him. At Chamonix the rule is that the guides are employed in turn, so that the absurd spectacle is possible of a man of real experience carrying a lady's shawl across the Mer de Glace, while a guide, who is little better than a porter, sets out to climb the Aiguille de Dru! However, the exceptions to this rule make a broad way of escape, for a lady alone, a member of an Alpine club, or a climber bent on a particularly difficult ascent, may choose a guide.

The pay of a first-class guide is seldom by tariff, for the class of climber who alone would have the opportunity of securing the services of one of the extremely limited number of guides of the first order generally engages him for some weeks at a time. Indeed, such men are usually bespoken a year in advance. The pay offered and expected is 25 fr. a day, including all expeditions, or else 10 fr. a day for rest days, 50 fr. for a peak, 25 fr. for a pass, in both cases the guide to keep himself, while travelling expenses and food on expeditions are to be paid for by the employer. If a season is fine and the party energetic, the former rate of payment may be the cheaper. The second guide generally receives two-thirds as much as the first guide.

When a novice is about to choose a guide, the advice of an experienced friend is invaluable, but, failing this, it is worse than useless to rely on inn-keepers, casual travellers, or the *guide-chef* at the guides' office of the locality. From these you can obtain the names of guides whom they recommend, but before making any definite arrangements, see the men themselves and carefully examine their books of certificates. In these latter lie your security, if you read them intelligently. Bear in mind that their value consists in their being signed by competent mountaineers. For instance, you may find something like the following in a guide's book:—

> A. Dumkopf took me up the Matterhorn to-day. He showed wonderful sureness of foot and steadiness of head, and I consider him a first-class guide, and have pleasure in recommending him.
>
> (Signed) A. S. SMITH.

Now, this is by some one you never heard of, and a very little consideration will show you that A. S. Smith is quite ignorant of climbing, judging by his wording of the certificate. That which follows, taken from the late Christian Almer's *Führerbuch*, is the sort of thing to carry weight:—

> Christian Almer has been our guide for three weeks, during which time we made the ascents of the Matterhorn (ascending by the northern and descending by the southern route), Weisshorn (from the Bies Glacier), Dent Blanche, and the Bietschhorn. Every journey that we take under Almer's guidance confirms us in the high opinion we have formed of his qualities as a guide and as a man. To the utmost daring and courage he unites prudence and foresight, seldom found in combination.
>
> (Signed) W. A. B. COOLIDGE.
>
> Visp, September 22nd, 1871.

It is when things go badly that a first-class guide is so conspicuously above an inferior man. In sudden storms or fog you may, if accompanied by the former, be in security, while the latter may get his party into positions of great peril. The former will take you slowly and carefully, sounding, perhaps, at every step, over what appears to you a perfectly easy snow plateau. The latter goes across a similar place unsuspecting of harm and with the rope loose, and, lo and behold, you all find yourselves in a hidden crevasse, and are lucky if you escape with your lives. In the early days of mountaineering guides were frequently drawn from the chamois hunters of a district, a sport requiring, perhaps, rather the quickness and agility of the born climber and gymnast than the qualities of calculation and prudence needed in addition by the guide.

A careful party descending a Rock Peak near Zermatt (the Unter Gabelhorn).

The most thoroughly unorthodox beginning to a great career of which I have ever heard was that of Joseph Imboden, of St Nicholas. When a boy his great desire, as he has often told me, was to become a guide. But his father would not consent to it, and apprenticed him to a boot-maker. During the time he toiled at manufacturing and mending shoes he contrived to save 20 fr. He then, at the age of sixteen, ran away from his employer, bought a note-book, and established himself at the Riffel Hotel above Zermatt. On every possible occasion he urged travellers to employ him as guide.

"Where is your book, young man?" they invariably enquired.

He showed it to them, but the pages were blank, and so no one would take him.

"At last," Imboden went on, "my 20 fr. were all but spent, when I managed to persuade a young Englishman to let me take him up Monte Rosa. I told him I knew the mountain well, and I would not charge him high. So we started. I had never set foot on a glacier before or on any mountain, but there was a good track up the snow, and I followed this, and there were other parties on Monte Rosa, so I copied what the guides did, and roped my gentleman as I saw the guides doing theirs. It was a lovely day, and we got on very well, and my gentleman was much pleased, and offered me an engagement to go to Chamonix with him over high passes.

"Then I said to myself: 'Lies have been very useful till now, but the time has come to speak the truth, and I will do so.'

"So I said to him: 'Herr, until to-day I have never climbed a mountain, but I am strong and active, and I have lived among mountaineers and mountains, and I am sure I can satisfy you if you will take me.'

"He was quite ready to do so, and we crossed the Col du Géant and went up Mont Blanc, but could do no more as the weather was bad. Then he wrote a great deal in my book, and since then I have never been in want of a gentleman to guide."

Imboden's eldest son, Roman, began still younger. When only thirteen he was employed by a member of the Alpine Club, Mr G. S. Barnes, to carry his lunch on the picnics he made with his friends on the glaciers near Saas-Fée. The party eventually undertook more ambitious expeditions, and one evening, Roman, who was very small for his age, was seen entering his native village at the head of a number of climbers who had crossed the Ried Pass, the little boy proudly carrying the largest knapsack of which he could possess himself, a huge coil of rope, and an ice-axe nearly as big as himself. Thus commenced the career of an afterwards famous Alpine guide.

During some fifteen seasons Imboden accompanied me on my climbs, frequently with Roman as second guide. Once the latter went with me to Dauphiné, and, though only twenty-three at the time, took me up the Meije, Ecrins, and other big peaks, his father being detained at home by reason of a bitter feud with the railway company about to run a line through his farm. It is sad to look back to the terrible ending of Roman's career at a period when he was the best young guide in the Alps. How little, in September 1895, as with the Imbodens, father and son, I stood on the summit of the Lyskamm, did any of us think that never again should we be together on a mountain, and that from the very peak on which we were Roman would be precipitated in one awful fall of hundreds of feet, his companions, Dr Guntner and the second guide Ruppen, also losing their lives.

I shall never forget the evening the news reached us at Zermatt. Imboden was, as usual, my guide, but Roman was leading guide to Dr Guntner. A month or two previously this gentleman had written to Roman asking if he would climb with him. Roman showed the letter to his father, saying: "I only go with English people, so I shall refuse." "Do not reply in a hurry," was the answer; "wait and see what the Herr is like, he is coming here soon." So Roman waited, saw Dr Guntner, liked him immensely, and engaged himself, not only till the end of the season, but also for a five months' mountaineering expedition in the Himalayas. We had all arrived at Zermatt from Fée a few days before, and while we waited in the valley for good weather, Dr Guntner, Roman Imboden, and Ruppen went to the Monte Rosa Hut to get some exercise next day on one of the easier peaks in the neighbourhood. Dr Guntner much wished to try the Lyskamm. Roman was against it, as the weather and snow were bad. However, in the morning there was a slight improvement, and as Dr Guntner was still most anxious to attempt the Lyskamm and Roman was so attached to him that he wished to oblige him in every way he could, he consented to, at any rate, go and look at it. Another party followed, feeling secure in the wake of such first-rate climbers, and, though the snow was atrocious and the weather grew worse and worse, no one turned back, and the summit was not far distant.

The gentleman in the second party did not feel very well, and made a long halt on the lower part of the ridge. Something seems to have aroused his suspicions—some drifting snow above, it was said, but I could never understand this part of the story—and an accident was feared. Abandoning the ascent, partly because of illness, partly on account of the weather, the party went down. At the bottom of the ridge, wishing to see if indeed something had gone wrong, they bore over towards the Italian side of the mountain. Directly the snowy plain at the base of the peak became visible, their worst fears were confirmed, for they perceived three black specks lying close together. Examining them through their glasses, it was but too certain that what they saw were the lifeless bodies of Dr Gunnter, Roman, and Ruppen.

Meanwhile, unconscious of the awful tragedy being enacted that day on the mountains, I had sent Imboden down to St Nicholas to see his family, and, after dinner, was sitting writing in the little salon of the Hotel Zermatt when two people entered, remarking to each other, "What a horrible smash on the Lyskamm!"

I started to my feet. Something told me it must be Roman's party. Crossing quickly over to the Monte Rosa Hotel, I found a silent crowd gathering in the street. I went into the office.

"Who is it?" I asked.

"Roman's party," was the answer.

"How do you know?"

"The other party has telephoned from the Riffel; we wait for them to arrive to hear particulars."

The crowd grew larger and larger in the dark without. All waited in cruel suspense. I could not bear to think of Imboden.

An hour passed. Then there was a stir among the waiting throng, and I went out among them and waited too.

The other party was coming. As the little band filed through the crowd, one question only was whispered.

"Is there any hope?" Sadly shaking their heads, the gentleman and his guides passed into Herr Seiler's room, and there we learned all there was to hear.

I need not dwell on Imboden's grief. He will never be the same man again, though three more sons are left him; but I must put on record his first words to me when I saw him: "Ruppen has left a young wife and several children, and they are very poor. Will you get up a subscription for them, ma'am, and help them as much as possible?"

STOPPED BY A BIG CREVASSE.

The party descended a little till a better passage was found by crossing a snow-bridge (page 37).

THE GENTLE PERSUASION OF THE ROPE (page 39).

It was done, and for Roman a tombstone was erected, "By his English friends, as a mark of their appreciation of his sterling qualities as a man and a guide." Roman was twenty-seven at the time of the accident. Neither Imboden nor I cared to face the sad associations of the Alps after the death of Roman, and the next and following years we mountaineered in Norway instead.

It will have been noticed that a climber nearly always takes two guides on an expedition. A visitor at Zermatt, or some other climbing centre, was heard to enquire: "Why do people take two guides? Is it in case they lose one?"

There are several reasons why a climbing party should not number less than three. In a difficult place, if one slips, his two companions should be able to check his fall immediately, whereas if the party number but two the risk of an accident is much greater. Again, a mishap to one of a party of two is infinitely more serious than had there been three climbing together. A glance at the accompanying photograph of some mountaineers reconnoitring a big crevasse will make my point clear.

A first-class guide will use the rope very differently to an inferior man, who allows it to hang about in a tangle, and to catch on every point of projecting rock.

A friend of mine, a Senior Wrangler, was extremely anxious to learn how to use a rope properly. So, instead of watching the method of his guide, he purchased a handbook, and learned by heart all the maxims therein contained on the subject. Shortly after these studies of his I was descending a steep face of rock in his company. I was in advance, and had gone down as far as the length of rope between us permitted. A few steps below was a commodious ledge, so I called out: "More rope, please!"

My friend hesitated, cleared his throat, and replied: "I am not sure if I ought to move just now, because, in *Badminton*, on page so-and-so, line so-and-so, the writer says——"

"Will you please give the lady more rope, sir!" called out Imboden.

"He says that if a climber finds himself in a position——"

"Will you go on, sir, or must I come down and help you?" exclaimed Imboden from above, and, at last, reluctantly enough, my friend moved on. He is now a distinguished member of the Alpine Club, so there is, perhaps, something to be said in favour of learning mountaineering from precept rather than example!

Occasionally a guide's manipulation of the rope includes something more arduous than merely being always ready to stop a slip. If his traveller is tired and the snow slopes are long and wearisome, it may happen that a guide will put the rope over his shoulder and pull his gentleman. A mountaineer of my acquaintance met a couple ascending the Breithorn in this manner. It was a hot day, and the amateur was very weary. Furthermore, he could speak no German. So he entreated his compatriot to intercede for him with the guide, who would insist on taking him up in spite of his groans of fatigue.

"Why do you not return when the gentleman wishes it?" queried the stranger.

"Sir," replied the guide, "he can go, he must go; he has paid me in advance!"

The rope generally used by climbers is made in England, is known as Alpine Club rope, and may be recognised by the bright red thread which runs through the centre of it. A climber should have his own rope, and not trust to any of doubtful quality.

Should climbers desire to make ascents in seldom explored parts of the world, such as the Caucasus, the Andes, or the Himalayas, they must take Alpine guides with them, for mountains everywhere have many characteristics in common, and as a good rider will go over a country unknown to him better than a bad horseman to whom it is familiar, so will a skilful guide find perhaps an easy way up a mountain previously unexplored, while the natives of the district declare the undertaking an impossible one. The Canadian Pacific Railway Company have recognised the truth of this, and have secured the services of Swiss guides for climbing in the Rockies.

The devotion of a really trustworthy guide to his employer is a fine trait in his character. My guide, Joseph Imboden, has often told me that for years the idea that he might somehow return safe from an expedition during which his traveller was killed, was simply a nightmare to him. Directly the rope was removed his anxiety commenced, and he was just as careful to see that the climber did not slip in an easy place as he had been on the most difficult part of the ascent. It is an unbroken tradition that no St. Nicholas guide ever comes home without his employer; all return safely or all are killed. Alas! the list of killed is a long one from that little Alpine village. In the churchyard, from the most recent grave, covered by the beautiful white marble stone placed there by Roman's English friends, to those recalling accidents a score or more of years ago, there lies the dust of many brave men. But I must not dwell on the gloom of the hills; let me rather recall some of the many occasions when a guide, by his skill, quickness, or resource, has saved his own and his charges' lives.

A famous Oberlander, Lauener by name, noted for his great strength, performed on one occasion a marvellous feat. He was ascending a steep ice slope, at the bottom of which was a precipice. He was alone with his "gentleman," and to this fact, usually by no means a desirable one, they both owed their lives. A big boulder seemed to be so deeply imbedded in the ice as to be actually part of the underlying rock. The traveller was just below it, the guide had cut steps alongside, and was above with, most happily, the rope taut. As he gained the level of the boulder he put his foot on it. To his horror it began to move! He took one rapid step back, and with a superhuman effort positively swung his traveller clean out of the steps and dangled him against the slope while the rock, heeling slowly outwards, broke loose from its icy fetters and plunged down the mountain side, right across the very place where the climber had been standing but an instant before.

A small man, whose muscles are in perfect condition, and who knows how to turn them to account, can accomplish what would really appear to be almost impossible for any one of his size.

Ulrich Almer, eldest son of the famous guide, the late Christian Almer, saved an entire party on one occasion by his own unaided efforts. They were descending the Ober Gabelhorn, a high mountain near Zermatt, and had reached a ridge where there is usually a large cornice. Now, a cornice is an overhanging eave of snow which has been formed by the wind blowing across a ridge. Sometimes cornices reach an enormous size, projecting 50 feet or more from the ridge. In climbing, presence of mind may avail much if a cornice breaks—absence of body is, however, infinitely preferable. Even first-class guides may err in deciding whether a party is or is not at an absolutely safe distance from a cornice. Though not actually on that part of the curling wave of snow which overhangs a precipice, the party may be in danger, for when a cornice breaks away it usually takes with it part of the snow beyond.

A typical Couloir is seen streaking the peak from summit to base in the centre of the picture ([page 73](#)).

THE WRONG WAY TO DESCEND.

The Cross marks the spot where the accident happened on the cornice of the Ober Gabelhorn in 1880 (page 43).

Very soft Snow which, on a steep slope, would cause an Avalanche (page 60).

By some miscalculation the first people on the rope walked on to the cornice. It broke, and they dropped straight down the precipice below. But at the same moment Ulrich saw and grasped the situation, and, springing right out on the other side, was able to check them in their terrible fall. It was no easy matter for the three men, one of whom had dislocated his shoulder, to regain the ridge, although held all the time by Ulrich. Still it was at length safely accomplished. The two gentlemen were so grateful to their guide that they wished to give him an acceptable present, and after much consideration decided that they could not do better than present him with a cow!

In trying to save a party which has fallen off a ridge, either by the breaking of a cornice or by a slip, I am told by first-rate guides that the proper thing to do is to jump straight out into the air on the opposite side. You thus bring a greater strain on the rope, and are more likely to check the pace at which your companions are sliding. I had a very awkward experience myself on one occasion when, owing to the softness of the snow, we started an avalanche, and the last guide, failing to spring over on the other side, we were all carried off our feet. Luckily, we were able, by thrusting our axes through into a lower and harder layer of snow, to arrest our wild career.

Piz Palü, in the Engadine, was once nearly the scene of a terrible tragedy through the breaking of a cornice, the party only being saved by the quickness and strength of one of their guides. The climbers consisted of Mrs Wainwright, her brother-in-law Dr B. Wainwright and the famous Pontresina guides Hans and Christian Grass. Bad weather overtook them during their ascent, and while they were passing along the ridge the fog was so thick that Hans Grass, who was leading, got on to the cornice. He was followed by the two travellers, and then with a mighty crack the cornice split asunder and precipitated them down the icy precipice seen to the right. Last on the rope came sturdy old Christian Grass, who grasped the awful situation in an instant, and sprang back. He held, but could, of course, do no more. Now was the critical time for the three hanging against the glassy wall. Both Hans and the lady had dropped their axes. Dr Wainwright alone retained his, and to this the party owed their lives. Of course he, hanging at the top, could do nothing; but after shouting out his intentions to those below, he called on Hans to make ready to catch the axe when it should slip by him. A moment of awful suspense, and the weapon was grasped by the guide, who forthwith hewed a big step out of the ice, and, standing on it, began the toilsome work of constructing a staircase back to the ridge. At last it was done, and when the three lay panting on the snow above, it was seen that by that time one strand only of the rope had remained intact.

The dotted line in the top right-hand corner shows the spot on Piz Palü where the Wainwright accident took place, the slope being the one the party fell down.

HANS AND CHRISTIAN GRASS.

The following account of a narrow escape from the result of a cornice breaking has an especially sad interest, for it was found amongst the papers of Lord Francis Douglas after his tragic death on the Matterhorn, and was addressed to the Editor of the *Alpine Journal*. The ascent described was made on 7th July 1865, and the poor young man was killed on the 14th of the same month.

The Gabelhorn is a fine peak, 13,365 feet high, in the Zermatt district.

Lord Francis Douglas writes:—"We arrived at the summit at 12.30. There we found that some one had been the day before, at least to a point very little below it, where they had built a cairn; but they had not gone to the actual summit, as it was a peak of snow, and there were no marks of footsteps. On this peak we sat down to dine, when, all of a sudden, I felt myself go, and the whole top fell with a crash thousands of feet below, and I with it, as far as the rope allowed (some 12 feet). Here, like a flash of lightning, Taugwald came right by me some 12 feet more; but the other guide, who had only the minute before walked a few feet from the summit to pick up something, did not go down with the mass, and thus held us both. The weight on the rope must have been about 23 stone, and it is wonderful that, falling straight down without anything to break one's fall, it did not break too. Joseph Viennin then pulled us up, and we began the descent to Zermatt."

Here, again, one of the guides saved the party from certain destruction.

It is in time of emergency that a really first-rate guide is so far ahead of an inferior man. In many cases when fatal results have followed unexpected bad weather or exceptionally difficult conditions of a mountain, bad guiding is to blame, while the cases when able guides have brought down themselves and their employers from very tight places indeed, are far more frequent than have ever been related.

A really wonderful example of a party brought safely home after terrible exposure is related in *The Pioneers of the Alps*. The well-known guides, Andreas Maurer and Emile Rey, with an English climber, had tried to reach the summit of the Aiguille du Plan by the steep ice slopes above the Chamonix Valley. "After step-cutting all day, they reached a point when to proceed was impossible, and retreat looked hopeless. To add to their difficulties, bad weather came on, with snow and intense cold. There was nothing to be done but to remain where they were for the night, and, if they survived it, to attempt the descent of the almost precipitous ice-slopes they had with such difficulty ascended. They stood through the long hours of that bitter night, roped together, without daring to move, on a narrow ridge, hacked level with their ice-axes. I know from each member of the party that they looked upon their case as hopeless, but Maurer not only never repined, but affected rather to like the whole thing, and though his own back was frozen hard to the ice-wall against which he leaned, and in spite of driving snow and numbing cold, he opened coat, waistcoat and shirt, and through the long hours of the night he held, pressed against his bare chest, the half-frozen body of the traveller who had urged him to undertake the expedition.

"The morning broke, still and clear, and at six o'clock, having thawed their stiffened limbs in the warm sun, they commenced the descent. Probably no finer feat in ice-work has ever been performed than that accomplished by Maurer and Rey on the 10th August 1880. It took them ten hours of continuous work to reach the rocks and safety, and their work was done without a scrap of food, after eighteen hours of incessant toil on the previous day, followed by a night of horrors such as few can realize." Had the bad weather continued, the party could not possibly have descended alive, "and this act of unselfish devotion would have remained unrecorded!"

Perhaps the most remarkable instance of endurance took place on the Croda Grande. The party consisted of Mr Oscar Schuster and the Primiero guide,

Giuseppe Zecchini. They set out on 17th March 1900, from Gosaldo at 5.10 A.M., the weather becoming unsettled as they went along. After they had been seven hours on the march a storm arose, yet, as they were within three-quarters of an hour of the top of their peak, they did not like to turn back. They duly gained the summit, the storm momentarily increasing in violence, and then they descended on the other side of the mountain till they came to an overhanging rock giving a certain amount of shelter. The guide had torn his gloves to pieces during the ascent, and his fingers were raw and sore from the difficult icy rocks he had climbed. As the cold was intense, they now began to be very painful. The weather grew worse and worse, and the two unfortunate climbers were obliged to remain in a hole scooped out of the snow, not only during the night of the 17th, but also during the whole day and night of the 18th. On the 19th, at 8 A.M., they made a start, not having tasted food for forty-eight hours. Five feet of snow had fallen, and the weather was still unsettled, but go they had to. First they tried to return as they came, but the masses of snow barred the way. They were delayed so long by the terrible state of the mountain that they had to spend another night out, and it was not till 6 P.M. on the 20th, after great danger that they reached Gosaldo. The guide, from whose account in *The Alpine Journal* I have borrowed, lost three fingers of his right hand and one of the left from frost-bite; the traveller appears to have come off scot free.

CHAPTER V

THE GUIDES OF THE ALPS—(*continued*).

The fathers of modern mountaineering were undoubtedly the two great Oberland guides, Melchior Anderegg and Christian Almer, who commenced their careers more than half a century ago. The former is still with us, the latter passed away some two years ago, accomplishing with ease expeditions of first-rate importance till within a season or two of his death. Melchior began his climbing experiences when filling the humble duties of boots at the Grimsel Inn. He was sent to conduct parties to the glaciers, his master taking the fee, while Melchior's share was the *pourboire*. His aptitude for mountain craft was soon remarked by the travellers whom he accompanied, and in a lucky hour for him—and indeed for all concerned—he was regularly taken into the employ of Mr Walker and his family. At that time Melchior could speak only a little German in addition to his Oberland *patois*, and was quite unaccustomed to intercourse with English people. He was most anxious, however, to say the right thing, and thought he could not do better than copy the travellers, so Mr Walker was somewhat startled on finding himself addressed as "Pa-pa," while his children were greeted respectively as "Lucy" and "Horace." The friendship between Melchior and the surviving members of Mr Walker's family has lasted ever since, and is worthy of all concerned. Melchior was born a guide, as he was born a gentleman, and no one who has had the pleasure of his acquaintance can fail to be impressed by his tact and wonderful sweetness of disposition, which have enabled him to work smoothly and satisfactorily with other guides, who might well have felt some jealousy at his career of unbroken success.

Melchior's great rival and friend, Christian Almer, was of a more impetuous disposition, but none the less a man to be respected and liked for his sturdy uprightness and devotion to his employers. The romantic tale of his ascent of the Wetterhorn, which first brought him into notice, has been admirably told by Chief-Justice Wills in his "Wanderings among the High Alps." Mr Wills, as he then was, had set out from Grindelwald to attempt the ascent of the hitherto unclimbed Wetterhorn. He had with him the guides Lauener, Bohren, and Balmat. The former, a giant in strength and height, had determined to mark the ascent in a way there should be no mistaking, so, seeking out the blacksmith, he had a "Flagge," as he termed it, prepared, and with this upon his back, he joined the rest of the party. The "Flagge" was a sheet of iron, 3 feet long and 2 broad, with rings to attach it to a bar of the same metal 10 or

12 feet high, which he carried in his hand. "He pointed first to the 'Flagge,' and then, with an exulting look on high, set up a shout of triumph which made the rocks ring again."

The Wetterhorn is so well seen from Grindelwald that it was natural some jealousy should arise as to who should first gain the summit. At this time Christian Almer was a chamois hunter, and his fine climbing abilities had been well trained in that difficult sport. He heard of the expedition, and took his measures accordingly.

Meanwhile Mr Wills' party, having bivouacked on the mountain side, had advanced some way upwards towards their goal, and were taking a little rest. As they halted, "we were surprised," writes Mr Wills, "to behold two other figures, creeping along the dangerous ridge of rocks we had just passed. They were at some little distance from us, but we saw they were dressed in the guise of peasants."

Lauener exclaimed that they must be chamois hunters, but a moment's reflection showed them that no chamois hunter would come that way, and immediately after they noticed that one of them "carried on his back a young fir-tree, branches, leaves, and all." This young man was Christian Almer, and a fitting beginning it was to a great career.

"We had turned aside to take our refreshment," continues Mr Wills, "and while we were so occupied they passed us, and on our setting forth again, we saw them on the snow slopes, a good way ahead, making all the haste they could, and evidently determined to be the first at the summit."

The Chamonix guides were furious, declaring that no one at Chamonix would be capable of so mean an action, and threatening an attack if they met them. The Swiss guides also began to see the enormity of the offence. "A great shouting now took place between the two parties, the result of which was that the piratical adventurers promised to wait for us on the rocks above, whither we arrived very soon after them. They turned out to be two chamois hunters, who had heard of our intended ascent, and resolved to be even with us, and plant their tree side by side with our 'Flagge.' They had started very early in the morning, had crept up the precipices above the upper glacier of Grindelwald before it was light, had seen us soon after daybreak, followed on our trail, and hunted us down. Balmat's anger was soon appeased when he found they owned the reasonableness of his desire that they should not steal from us the distinction of being the first to scale that awful peak, and instead of administering the fisticuffs he had talked about, he declared they were '*bons enfants*' after all, and presented them with a cake of chocolate; thus the pipe of peace was smoked, and tranquility reigned between the rival forces."

The two parties now moved upwards together, and eventually reached the steep final slope of snow so familiar to all who have been up the Wetterhorn. They could not tell what was above it, but they hoped and thought it might be the top.

CHRISTIAN ALMER, 1894.

At last, after cutting a passage through the cornice, which hung over the slope like the crest of a great wave about to break, Mr Wills stepped on to the ridge. His description is too thrilling to be omitted. "The instant before, I had been face to face with a blank wall of ice. One step, and the eye took in a boundless expanse of crag and glacier, peak and precipice, mountain and valley, lake and plain. The whole world seemed to lie at my feet. The next moment, I was almost appalled by the awfulness of our position. The side we had come up was steep; but it was a gentle slope compared with that which now fell away from where I stood. A few yards of glittering ice at our feet, and then nothing between us and the green slopes of Grindelwald, 9000 feet below. Balmat told me afterwards that it was the most awful and startling moment he had known in the course of his long mountain experience. We felt as in the immediate presence of Him who had reared this tremendous pinnacle, and beneath the 'majestical roof' of whose blue heaven we stood poised, as it seemed, half-way beneath the earth and sky."

Another notable ascent by Almer of the Wetterhorn was made exactly thirty years later, when, with the youngest of his five sons (whom he was taking up for the first time) and an English climber he repeated as far as possible all the details of his first climb, the lad carrying a young fir-tree, as his father had done, to plant on the summit. Finally, in 1896, Almer celebrated his golden wedding on the top of the mountain he knew so well. He was accompanied by his wife, and the sturdy old couple were guided by their sons.

But all guides are not the Melchiors or the Almers of their profession. Sometimes, bent on photography from the easier peaks, I have taken whoever was willing to come and carry the camera, and on one occasion had rather an amusing experience with an indifferent specimen of the Pontresina *Führerverein*. All went well at first, and our large party, mostly of friends who knew nothing of climbing, trudged along quite happily till after our first halt for food. When we started again after breakfast our first adventure occurred. We had one first-class guide with us in the person of Martin Schocker, but were obliged to make up the number required for the gang by pressing several inferior men into our service. One of these was leading the first rope-full (if such an expression may be allowed), and with that wonderful capacity for discovering crevasses where they would be avoided by more skilful men, he walked on to what looked like a firm, level piece of snow, and in a second was gone! The rope ran rapidly out as we flung ourselves into positions of security, and as we had kept our proper distances the check came on us all as on one. We remained as we were, while the second caravan advanced to our assistance. Its leading guide, held by the others, cautiously approached the hole, and seeing that our man was dangling, took measures to haul him up. This was not very easy, as the rope had cut deeply into the soft snow at the edge; but with so large a party there was no real difficulty in effecting a rescue. At last our guide appeared, very red in the face, puffing like a grampus, and minus his hat. As soon as he had regained breath he began to talk very fast indeed. It seemed that the crown of his hat was used by him for purposes similar to those served by the strong rooms and safes of the rich; for in his head-gear he was in the habit of storing family documents of value, and among others packed away there was his marriage certificate! The hat now reposed at the bottom of a profound crevasse, and his lamentations were, in consequence, both loud and prolonged. I don't know what happened when he got home, but for the rest of the day he was a perfect nuisance to us all, explaining by voice and gesture, repeated at every halt, the terrifying experience and incalculable loss he had suffered. Another unlucky result of his dive into the crevasse was its effect upon a lady member of the party, who had been induced, by much persuasion, to venture for the first time on a mountain. So startled was she by his sudden disappearance, that she jibbed determinedly at every crack in the glacier we had to cross, and, as they were many, our progress became slower and slower, and it was very late indeed before we regained the valley.

Mr Clinton Dent, writing in *The Alpine Journal*, justly remarks: "Guides of the very first rank are still to be found, though they are rare; yet there are, perhaps, as many of the first rank now as there have ever been. The demand is so prodigiously great now that the second-class guide, or the young fully qualified guide who has made some little reputation for brilliancy, is often employed as leader on work which may easily overtax his powers. There is no more pressing question at the present time in connection with mountaineering, than the proper training of young guides."

The dust of an Avalanche falling from the Matterhorn Glacier may be seen to the right.

CHAPTER VI

AN AVALANCHE ON THE HAUT-DE-CRY

The Haut-de-Cry is not one of the giants of the Alps. It is a peak of modest height but fine appearance, rising abruptly from the valley of the Rhone. In 1864 it had never been climbed in winter, and one of our countrymen, Mr Philip Gosset, set out in February of that year to attempt its ascent. He had with him a friend, Monsieur Boissonnet, the famous guide Bennen, and three men from a village, named Ardon, close by, who were to act as local guides or porters.

The party had gained a considerable height on the mountain when it became necessary to cross a couloir or gully filled with snow. It was about 150 feet broad at the top, and 400 or 500 at the bottom. "Bennen did not seem to like the look of the snow very much," writes Mr Gosset in *The Alpine Journal*. "He asked the local guides whether avalanches ever came down this couloir, to which they answered that our position was perfectly safe. We were walking in the following order—Bevard, Nance, Bennen, myself, Boissonnet, and Rebot. Having crossed over about three-quarters of the breadth of the couloir, the two leading men suddenly sank considerably above their waists. Bennen tightened the rope. The snow was too deep to think of getting out of the hole they had made, so they advanced one or two steps, dividing the snow with their bodies. Bennen turned round and told us he was afraid of starting an avalanche; we asked whether it would not be better to return and cross the couloir higher up. To this the three Ardon men opposed themselves; they mistook the proposed precaution for fear, and the two leading men continued their work.

"After three or four steps gained in the aforesaid manner, the snow became hard again. Bennen had not moved—he was evidently undecided what he should do. As soon, however, as he saw hard snow again, he advanced, and crossed parallel to, but above, the furrow the Ardon men had made. Strange to say, the snow supported him. While he was passing, I observed that the leader, Bevard, had ten or twelve feet of rope coiled round his shoulder. I of course at once told him to uncoil it, and get on to the arête, from which he was not more than fifteen feet distant. Bennen then told me to follow. I tried his steps, but sank up to my waist in the very first. So I went through the furrows, holding my elbows close to my body, so as not to touch the sides. This furrow was about twelve feet long, and as the snow was good on the other side, we had all come to the false conclusion that the snow was accidentally softer there than elsewhere. Bennen advanced; he had made but a few steps when we heard a deep, cutting sound. The snow-field split in two, about fourteen or fifteen feet above us. The cleft was at first quite narrow, not more than an inch broad. An awful silence ensued; it lasted but a few seconds, and then it was broken by Bennen's voice, 'Wir sind alle verloren.'[1] His words were slow and solemn, and those who knew him felt what they really meant when spoken by such a man as Bennen. They were his last words. I drove my alpenstock into the snow, and brought the weight of my body to bear on it. I then waited. It was an awful moment of suspense. I turned my head towards Bennen to see whether he had done the same thing. To my astonishment I saw him turn round, face the valley, and stretch out both arms. The ground on which we stood began to move slowly, and I felt the utter uselessness of any alpenstock. I soon sank up to my shoulders, and began descending backwards. From this moment I saw nothing of what had happened to the rest of the party. With a good deal of trouble I succeeded in turning round. The speed of the avalanche increased rapidly, and before long I was covered up with snow. I was suffocating, when I suddenly came to the surface again. I was on a wave of the avalanche, and saw it before me as I was carried down. It was the most awful sight I ever saw. The head of the avalanche was already at the spot where we had made our last halt. The head alone was preceded by a thick cloud of snow-dust; the rest of the avalanche was clear. Around me I heard the horrid hissing of the snow, and far before me the thundering of the foremost part of the avalanche. To prevent myself sinking again, I made use of my arms, much in the same way as when swimming in a standing position. At last I noticed that I was moving slower; then I saw the pieces of snow in front of me stop at some yards distant; then the snow straight before me stopped, and I heard on a large scale the same creaking sound that is produced when a heavy cart passes over frozen snow in winter. I felt that I also had stopped, and instantly threw up both arms to protect my head, in case I should again be covered up. I had stopped, but the snow behind me was still in motion; its pressure on my body was so strong that I thought I should be crushed to death. This tremendous pressure lasted but a short time; I was covered up by snow coming from behind me. My first impulse was to try and uncover my head—but this I could not do, the avalanche had frozen by pressure the moment it stopped, and I was frozen in. Whilst trying vainly to move my arms, I suddenly became aware that the hands as far as the wrist had the faculty of motion. The conclusion was easy, they must be above the snow. I set to work as well as I could; it was time for I could not have held out much longer. At last I saw a faint glimmer of light. The crust above my head was getting thinner, but I could not reach it any more with my hands; the idea struck me that I might pierce it with my breath. After several efforts I succeeded in doing so, and felt suddenly a rush of air towards my mouth, I saw the sky again through a little round hole. A dead silence reigned around me; I was so surprised to be still alive, and so persuaded at the first moment that none of my fellow-sufferers had survived, that I did not even think of shouting for them. I then made vain efforts to extricate my arms, but found it impossible; the most I could do was to join the ends of my fingers, but they could not reach the snow any longer. After a few minutes I heard a man shouting; what a relief it was to know that I was not the sole survivor!—to know that perhaps he was not frozen in and could come to my assistance! I answered; the voice approached, but seemed uncertain where to go, and yet it was now quite near. A sudden exclamation of surprise! Rebot had seen my hands. He cleared my head in an instant, and was about to try and cut me out completely, when I saw a foot above the snow, and so near to me that I could touch it with my arms, although they were not quite free yet. I at once tried to move the foot; it was my poor friend's. A pang of agony shot through me as I saw that the foot did not move. Poor Boissonnet had lost sensation, and was perhaps already dead.

"Rebot did his best. After some time he wished me to help him, so he freed my arms a little more, so that I could make use of them. I could do but little, for Rebot had torn the axe from my shoulder as soon as he had cleared my head (I generally carry an axe separate from my alpenstock—the blade tied to the belt, and the handle attached to the left shoulder). Before coming to me Rebot had helped Nance out of the snow; he was lying nearly horizontally, and was not much covered over. Nance found Bevard, who was upright in the snow, but covered up to the head. After about twenty minutes, the two last-named guides came up. I was at length taken out; the snow had to be cut with the axe down to my feet before I could be pulled out. A few minutes after 1 P.M. we came to my poor friend's face.... I wished the body to be taken out completely, but nothing could induce the three guides to work any longer, from the moment they saw it was too late to save him. I acknowledge that they were nearly as incapable of doing anything as I was. When I was taken out of the snow the cord had to be cut. We tried the end going towards Bennen, but could not move it; it went nearly straight down, and showed us that there was the grave of the bravest guide the Valais ever had or ever will have."

Thus ends one of the most magnificent descriptions of an avalanche which has ever been written. The cause of the accident was a mistaken opinion as to the state of winter snow, which is very different to the snow met with in summer, and of which at that time the best guides had no experience.

A RACE FOR LIFE

Once upon a time, in the year 1872, a certain famous mountaineer, Mr F. F.

Tuckett, had with his party a desperate race for life. The climbers numbered five in all, three travellers and two guides, and had started from the Wengern Alp to ascend the Eiger. Nowadays there is a railway to the Wengern Alp, and so thousands of English people are familiar with the appearance of the magnificent group of mountains—the Eiger, the Mönch, and the Jungfrau—which they have before them as they pass along in the train. Suffice it here to say that the way up the Eiger lies over a glacier, partly fed by another high above it, from which, through a narrow, rocky gully, great masses of ice now and again come dashing down. Unless the fall is a very big one, climbers skirting along the edge of this glacier are safe enough, but on the only occasion I have been up the Eiger, I did not fancy this part of the journey.

Eiger.   Mönch.

FROM THE LAUBERHORN.

**The Cross marks the Scene of "A Race for Life."
The dotted line shows the steep Ice-Wall of the Eigerjoch (page 208).**

To return to Mr Tuckett and his friends. They were advancing up the snowy valley below the funnel-shaped opening through which an avalanche occasionally falls. The guide, Ulrich Lauener, was leading, and, remarks Mr Tuckett, "He is a little hard of hearing; and although his sight, which had become very feeble in 1870, is greatly improved, both ear and eye were perhaps less quick to detect any unexpected sound or movement than might otherwise have been the case. Be this as it may, when all of a sudden I heard a sort of crack somewhere up aloft, I believe that, for an instant or two, his was the only head not turned upwards in the direction from which it seemed to proceed, viz., the hanging ice-cliff; but the next moment, when a huge mass of sérac broke away, mingled apparently with a still larger contingent of snow from the slopes above, whose descent may, indeed, have caused, or at least hastened, the disruption of the glacier, every eye was on the look-out, though as yet there was no indication on the part of any one, nor I believe any thought for one or two seconds more, that we were going to be treated to anything beyond a tolerably near view of such an avalanche as it rarely falls to anyone's lot to see. Down came the mighty cataract, filling the couloir to its brim; but it was not until it had traversed a distance of 600 to 800 feet, and on suddenly dashing in a cloud of frozen spray over one of the principal rocky ridges with which, as I have said, the continuity of the snow-slope was broken, appeared as if by magic to triple its width, that the idea of danger to ourselves flashed upon me. I now perceived that its volume was enormously greater than I had at first imagined, and that, with the tremendous momentum it had by this time acquired, it might, instead of descending on the right between us and the rocks of the Klein Eiger, dash completely across the base of the Eiger itself in front of us, attain the foot of the Rothstock ridge, and then, trending round, sweep the whole surface of the glacier, ourselves included, with the besom of destruction.

"I instinctively bolted for the rocks of the Rothstock—if haply it might not be too late—yelling rather than shouting to the others, 'Run for your lives!'

"Ulrich was the last to take the alarm, though the nearest to the danger, and was thus eight or ten paces behind the rest of us, though he, too, shouted to Whitwell to run for his life directly he became aware of the situation. But by this time we were all straining desperately through the deep, soft snow for dear life, yet with faces turned upwards to watch the swift on-coming of the foe. I remember being struck with the idea that it seemed as though, sure of its prey, it wished to play with us for a while, at one moment letting us imagine that we had gained upon it, and were getting beyond the line of its fire, and the next, with mere wantonness of vindictive power, suddenly rolling out on its right a vast volume of grinding blocks and whirling snow, as though to show that it could out-flank us at any moment it chose.

"Nearer and nearer it came, its front like a mighty wave about to break, yet that still 'on the curl hangs poising'; now it has traversed the whole width of the glacier above us, taking a somewhat diagonal direction; and now run, oh, run! if ever you did, for here it comes straight at us, still outflanking us, swift, deadly, and implacable! The next instant we saw no more; a wild confusion of whirling snow and fragments of ice—a frozen cloud—swept over us, entirely concealing us from one another, and still we were untouched—at least I knew that I was—and still we ran. Another half second and the mist had passed, and there lay the body of the monster, whose head was still careering away at lightning speed far below us, motionless, rigid, and harmless. It will naturally be supposed that the race was one which had not admitted of being accurately timed by the performers; but I believe that I am speaking with precision when I say that I do not think the whole thing occupied from first to last more than five or six seconds. How narrow our escape was may be inferred from the fact that the spot where I halted for a moment to look back after it had passed, was found to be just twelve yards from its edge, and I don't think that in all we had had time to put more than thirty yards between us and the point where our wild rush for the rocks first began. Ulrich's momentary lagging all but cost him his life; for in spite of his giant stride and desperate exertions he only just contrived to fling himself forwards as the edge of the frozen torrent dashed past him. This may sound like exaggeration, but he assured me that he felt some fragments strike his legs; and it will perhaps appear less improbable when it is considered that he was certainly several yards in the rear, and when the avalanche came to a standstill, its edge, intersecting and concealing our tracks along a sharply defined line, rose rigid and perpendicular, like a wall of cyclopean masonry, as the old Bible pictures represent the waters of the Red Sea, standing 'upright as an heap' to let the Israelites through.

"The avalanche itself consisted of a mixture, in tolerably equal proportions, of blocks of sérac of all shapes and sizes, up to irregular cubes of four or five feet on a size, and snow thoroughly saturated with water—the most dangerous of all descriptions to encounter, as its weight is enormous. We found that it covered the valley for a length of about 3300 feet, and a maximum breadth of 1500, tailing off above and below to 500 or 1000 feet. Had our position on the slope been a few hundred feet higher or lower, or in other words, had we been five minutes earlier or later, we must have been caught beyond all chance of escape."

There was no rashness which can be blamed in the party finding themselves in the position described. Avalanches, when they fall down the gully, hardly ever come so far as the one met with on this occasion, and they very seldom fall at all in the early morning. The famous guide, Christian Almer, while engaged on another expedition, visited the spot after the avalanche had fallen, and said that it was the mightiest he had ever seen in his life. Mr Tuckett roughly estimated its total weight as about 450,000 tons.

CHAPTER VII

CAUGHT IN AN AVALANCHE ON THE MATTERHORN

The following exciting account is taken from an article by Herr Lorria, which appeared in *The St Moritz Post* for 28th January 1888. The injuries received were so terrible that, I believe, Herr Lorria never entirely ceased to feel their effects.

The party consisted of two Austrian gentlemen, Herren Lammer and Lorria, without guides, who, in 1887, had made Zermatt their headquarters for some climbs. They had difficulty in deciding which ascent to begin with, especially as the weather had recently been bad, and the peaks were not in first-class condition. Herr Lorria writes:

"I fancied the Pointe de Zinal as the object of our tour; but Lammer, who had never been on the Matterhorn, wished to climb this mountain by the western flank—a route which had only once before been attacked, namely by Mr Penhall. We had with us the drawing of Penhall's route, published in *The Alpine Journal*.

"After skirting a jutting cliff, we reached the couloir at its narrowest point. It was clear that we had followed the route laid down in *The Alpine Journal*; and although Mr Penhall says that the rocks here are very easy, I cannot at all agree with him.

"We could not simply cross over the couloir, for, on the opposite side, the rocks looked horrible: it was only possible to cross it some forty or fifty mètres higher. We climbed down into the couloir: the ice was furrowed by avalanches. We were obliged to cut steps as we mounted upwards in a sloping direction. In a quarter of an hour we were on the other side of the couloir. The impression which the couloir made upon me is best shown by the words which I at the moment addressed to Lammer: 'We are now completely cut off.' We saw clearly that it was only the early hour, before the sun was yet upon the couloir, which protected us from danger. Once more upon the rocks, we kept our course as much as possible parallel to the N.W. arête. We clambered along, first over rocks covered with ice, then over glassy ledges, always sloping downwards. Our progress was slow indeed; the formation of the rock surface was ever becoming more unfavourable, and the covering of ice was a fearful hindrance.

"Such difficult rocks I had rarely seen before; the wrinkled ledges of the Dent Blanche were easy compared to them. At 1 P.M., we were standing on a level with the "Grand Tower"; the summit lay close before us, but as far as we could see, the rocks were completely coated with a treacherous layer of ice. Immediately before us was a precipitous ice couloir. All attempts to advance were fruitless, even our crampons were of no avail. Driven back! If this, in all cases, is a heavy blow for the mountain climber, we had here, in addition, the danger which we knew so well, and which was every moment increasing. It was one o'clock in the afternoon; the rays of the sun already struck the western wall of the mountain; stone after stone, loosened from its icy fetters, whistled past us. Back! As fast as possible back! Lammer pulled off his shoes and I stuffed them into the knapsack, holding also our two ice-axes. As I clambered down the first I was often obliged to trust to the rope. The ledges, which had given us trouble in the ascent, were now fearfully difficult. Across a short ice slope, in which we had cut steps in the ascent, Lammer was obliged, as time pressed, to get along without his shoes. The difficulties increased; every moment the danger became greater; and already whole avalanches of stones rattled down. The situation was indeed critical. At last, after immense difficulty, we reached the edge of the couloir at the place we had left it in the ascent. But we could find no spot protected from the stones; they literally came down upon us like hail. Which was the more serious danger, the threatening avalanches in the couloir or the pelting of the stones which swept down from every side? On the far side of the couloir there was safety, as all the stones must in the end reach the couloir, which divides the whole face of the mountain into two parts. It was now five o'clock in the afternoon; the burning rays of the sun came down upon us, and countless stones whirled through the air. We remembered the saying of Dr Güssfeldt, in his magnificent description of the passage of the Col du Lion, that only at midnight is tranquility restored. We resolved, then, to risk the short stretch across the couloir. Lammer pulled on his shoes; I was the first to leave the rocks. The snow which covered the ice was suspiciously soft, but we had no need to cut steps. In the avalanche track before us on the right a mighty avalanche is thundering down; stones leap into the couloir, and give rise to new avalanches.

"Suddenly my consciousness is extinguished, and I do not recover it till twenty-one days later. I can, therefore, only tell what Lammer saw. Gently from above an avalanche of snow came sliding down upon us; it carried Lammer away in spite of his efforts, and it projected me with my head against a rock. Lammer was blinded by the powdery snow, and thought that his last hour was come. The thunder of the roaring avalanche was fearful; we were dashed over rocks, laid bare in the avalanche track, and leaped over two immense bergschrunds. At every change of the slope we flew into the air, and then were plunged again into the snow, and often dashed against one another.

For a long time it seemed to Lammer as if all were over, countless thoughts went thronging through his brain, until at last the avalanche had expended its force, and we were left lying on the Tiefenmatten Glacier. Our fall was estimated at from 550 to 800 English feet.

"I lay unconscious, quite buried in the snow; the rope had gone twice round my neck and bound it fast. Lammer, who quickly recovered consciousness, pulled me out of the snow, cut the rope, and gave me a good shake. I then awoke, but being delirious, I resisted with all my might my friend's endeavours to pull me out of the track of the avalanche. However, he succeeded in getting me on to a stone (I was, of course, unable to walk), and gave me his coat; and having thus done all that was possible for me, he began to creep downwards on hands and knees. He could not stand, having a badly sprained ankle; except for that he escaped with merely a few bruises and scratches. At length Lammer arrived at the Stockje hut, but to his intense disappointment there was nobody there. He did not pause to give vent to his annoyance, however, but continued his way down. Twice he felt nearly unable to proceed, and would have abandoned himself to his fate had not the thought of me kept him up and urged him on. At three o'clock in the morning he reached the Staffel Alp, but none of the people there were willing to venture on the glacier. He now gave up all hope that I could be saved, though he nevertheless sent a messenger to Herr Seiler, who reached Zermatt at about 4.15 A.M.

"In half an hour's time a relief party set out from Zermatt. When the party reached the Staffel Alp, Lammer was unconscious, but most fortunately he had written on a piece of paper the information that I was lying at the foot of Penhall's couloir. They found me about half-past eight o'clock. I had taken off all my clothes in my delirium, and had slipped off the rock on which Lammer had left me. One of my feet was broken and both were frozen into the snow, and had to be cut out with an axe.

"At 8 P.M. I was brought back to Zermatt, and for twenty days I lay unconscious at the Monte Rosa Hotel hovering between life and death."

Herr Lorria pays a warm tribute to the kindness of Seiler and his wife, and the skill of Dr de Courten, who saved his limbs when other doctors wished to amputate them. He ends his graphic account as follows: "The lesson to be learnt from our accident is not 'Always take guides,' but rather 'Never try the Penhall route on the Matterhorn, except after a long series of fine, hot days, for otherwise the western wall of the mountain is the most fearful mouse-trap in the Alps.'"

THE ICE AVALANCHE OF THE ALTELS.

Those who climbed in the Alps during the summer of 1895 will recollect how wonderfully dry and warm the weather was, denuding the mountains of snow and causing a number of rock-falls, so that many ascents became very dangerous, and, in my own case, after one or two risky encounters with falling stones, we decided to let the rock peaks alone for the rest of that campaign.

In the centre of the picture may be seen an Avalanche, which a non-climber might mistake for a Waterfall, dropping down the Rocks of the Wetterhorn.

In *The Alpine Journal* of August 1897, Mr Charles Slater gives an admirable description of a great ice-avalanche which overwhelmed one of the fertile pastures near the well-known Gemmi route. From this account I make some extracts, which will give an idea of the magnitude of the disaster and its unusual character, as the ice from a falling glacier rarely ever approaches cultivated land and dwellings.

The scene of the catastrophe was at Spitalmatten, a pasturage with châlets used in summer by the shepherds, in a basin at the beginning of the valley which extends to the pass. Steep slopes bound it on the east, and above them rises the glacier-capped peak of the Altels. The glacier was well seen from the Gemmi path, and all tourists who passed that way must have noticed and admired it. It is believed that a big crevasse, running right across the glacier, was noticed during the month of August, and the lower part of the glacier seemed to be completely cut off from the upper portion by it.

On the evening of 10th September, the Vice-President of the commune of Leuk (to which commune the Alp belonged) arrived at the châlets to settle the accounts of the past summer. Several of the women had already gone down, taking some of the calves with them, and the rest of the inhabitants of the little settlement were to follow next day. The weather was warm but cloudy, with a strong *föhn* wind.[2]

On the morning of 11th September, about 5 A.M., the few people who lived at or near the Schwarenbach Inn heard a roar like an earthquake, and felt a violent blast of wind. A servant, rushing out of the inn, saw "what appeared to be a white mist streaming down the Altel's slope. The huge mass of ice forming the lower end of the glacier had broken away, rushed down the mountain side, leapt from the Tateleu plateau into the valley, and, like an immense wave, had swept over the Alp, up the Uschinen Grat, as if up a 1500 sea-wall, and even sent its ice-foam over this into the distant Uschinen Thal."

The only other eye-witness of this appalling catastrophe was a traveller who was walking up the Kanderthal from Frutigen in the early morning. "He saw in the Gemmi direction a fearful whirlwind, with dust and snow-clouds, and experienced later a cold rain falling from a clear sky, the rain being probably due to the melting of the ice-cloud."

The scene after the disaster must have been a terrible one. "Winter had apparently come in the midst of summer"; the whole pasture was covered with masses of ice. "The body of the Vice-President was found lying 180 yards away from the hut. Another body had been flung into the branches of an uprooted tree, while a third was found still holding a stocking in one hand, having been killed in the act of dressing."

There was no chance of escape for the people, as only a minute or little more elapsed from the time the avalanche started till it reached the settlement. The cows were nearly all killed, "they seem to have been blown like leaves before a storm to enormous distances."

A year later, much of the avalanche was still unmelted.

The thickness of the slice of glacier which broke away is believed to have been about 25 feet, and it fell through a vertical height of 4700 feet. It moved at about the average rate of two miles a minute.

"It is difficult to realise these vast figures, and a few comparisons have been suggested which may help to give some idea of the forces which were called into play. The material which fell would have sufficed to bury the City of London to the depth of six feet, and Hyde Park and Kensington Gardens would have disappeared beneath a layer six-and-a-half feet deep. The enormous energy of the moving mass may be dimly pictured when we think that a weight of ice and stones ten times greater than the tonnage of the whole of England's battle-ships plunged on to the Alp at a speed of nearly 300 miles an hour."

An almost exactly similar accident had occurred in 1782.

AN AVALANCHE WHICH ROBBED A LADY OF A GARMENT

One of the greatest advantages in mountaineering as a sport is the amount of enjoyment it gives even when climbing-days are past. While actually engaged in the ascent of difficult peaks our minds are apt to be entirely engrossed with the problem of getting up and down them, but afterwards we delight in recalling every interesting passage, every glorious view, every successful climb; and perhaps this gives us even more pleasure than the experiences themselves.

If we happen to have combined photography with mountaineering we are particularly to be envied, for an hour in the company of one of our old albums will recall with wonderful vividness many an incident which we should have otherwise forgotten.

Turning over some prints which long have lain on one side, a wave of recollection brings before me some especially happy days on snowy peaks, and makes me long to bring a breath of Alpine air to the cities, where for so much of the year dwell many of my brother and sister climbers.

With the help of the accompanying photographs, which will serve to generally illustrate my remarks, let me relate what befell me during an ascent of the Schallihorn—a peak some twelve thousand and odd feet high, in the neighbourhood of Zermatt.

Now, although Zermatt is a very familiar playground for mountaineers, yet even as late as ten years ago one or two virgin peaks and a fair number of new and undesirable routes up others were still to be found. I had had my share of success on the former, and was at the time of which I write looking about for an interesting and moderately safe way, hitherto untrodden, up one of the lesser-known mountains in the district. My guide and my friend of many years, Joseph Imboden, racked his brains for a suitable novelty, and at length suggested that as no one had hitherto attacked the south-east face of the Schallihorn we might as well see if it could be ascended. He added that he was not at all sure if it was possible—a remark I have known him to make on more than one peak in far away Arctic Norway, when the obvious facility of an ascent had robbed it of half its interest. However, in those days I still rose satisfactorily to observations of that sort, and was at once all eagerness to set out. We were fortunate in securing as our second guide Imboden's brilliant son Roman, who happened to be disengaged just then. A further and little dreamed-of honour was in store for us, as on our endeavouring to hire a porter to take our things to the bivouac from the tiny village of Taesch no less a person than the mayor volunteered to accompany us in that capacity.

MR WHYMPER. ZERMATT, 1896.

MRS AUBREY LE BLOND ON A MOUNTAIN TOP.
Photographed by her Guide, Joseph Imboden

A Hot Day in Mid-Winter on the Summit of a Peak 13,000 feet high.

So we started upwards one hot afternoon, bound for some overhanging rocks, which, we were assured by those who had never visited the spot, we should find. For the regulation routes up the chief peaks the climber can generally count on a hut, where, packed in close proximity to his neighbours, he lies awake till it is time to get up, and sets forth on his ascent benefited only in imagination by his night's repose. Within certain limits the less a man is catered for the more comfortable he is, and the more he has to count on himself the better are the arrangements for his comfort. Thus I have found a well-planned bivouac under a great rock infinitely preferable to a night in a hut, and a summer's campaign in tents amongst unexplored mountains more really luxurious than a season in an over-thronged Alpine hotel.

Two or three hours' walking took us far above the trees and into the region of short grass and stony slopes. Eventually we reached a hollow at the very foot of our mountain, and here we began to look about for suitable shelter and a flat surface on which to lay the sleeping-bags. The pictured rocks of inviting appearance were nowhere to be found, and what there were offered very inferior accommodation. But the weather was perfect, and we had an ample supply of wraps, so we contented ourselves with what protection was given by a steep, rocky wall, and turned our attention to the Schallihorn. The proposed route could be well seen. Imboden traced out the way he intended taking for a long distance up the mighty precipice in front of us. There were tracks of avalanches at more than one spot, and signs of falling stones were not infrequent. My guide thought he could avoid all danger by persistently keeping to the projecting ridges, and his idea was to descend by whatever way we went up, as the ordinary route is merely a long, uninteresting grind.

We now lit a fire, made soup and coffee, and soon after got into our sleeping-bags. The night passed peacefully, save for the rumble of an occasional avalanche, when great masses of ice broke loose on the glacier hard by. Before dawn we were stirring, and by the weird light of a huge fire were making our preparations for departure. It gradually grew light as our little party moved in single file towards the rocky ramparts which threatened to bar the way to the upper world. As we ascended a stony slope, Imboden remarked, "Why, ma'am, you still have on that long skirt! Let us leave it here; we can pick it up on our return." Now, in order not to be conspicuous when starting for a climbing expedition, I always wore an ordinary walking-skirt over my mountaineering costume. It was of the lightest possible material, so that, if returning by a different route, it could be rolled up and carried in a knapsack. I generally started from the bivouac without it; but the presence on this occasion of the Mayor of Täsch had quite overawed me; hence the unusual elegance of my get-up. Lest I be thought to dwell at undue length on so trifling a matter, I may add that the skirt had adventures that day of so remarkable a nature that the disappearance of Elijah in his chariot can alone be compared to them.

The skirt was now duly removed, rolled up and placed under a heavy stone, which we marked with a small cairn, so as to find it the more easily on our return. Shortly after, the real climb began, and, putting on the rope, we commenced the varied series of gymnastics which make life worth living to the mountaineer. We had several particularly unpleasant gullies to cross, up which Imboden glanced hastily and suspiciously, and hurried us over, fearing the fall of stones. At length we came for a little time to easier ground, and as the day was now intensely hot the men took off their waistcoats, leaving them and their watches in a hole in the rock. Above this gentler slope the mountain steepened again, and a ridge in the centre, running directly upwards, alone gave a possible route to the summit. This ridge, at first broad and simple, before long narrowed to a knife-edge. There was always enough to hold; but the rocks were so loose and rotten that we hardly dared to touch them. Spread out over those treacherous rocks, adhering by every finger in our endeavour to distribute our weight, we slowly wormed ourselves upwards. Such situations are always trying. The most brilliant cragsman finds his skill of little avail. Unceasing care and patience alone can help him here. Throwing down the most insecure of the blocks, which fell sometimes on one side, sometimes on the other of the ridge, we gradually advanced. The conversation ran rather in a groove: "Not that one, ma'am, or the big fellow on the top will come down!"

"Don't touch the red one or the little white one!" "Now come up to where I am without stepping on any of them!" "Roman! look out! I'm letting this one go!" Then bang! bang! bang! and a disgusting smell as of gunpowder, while a great boulder dashed in leaps towards the glacier below, grinding and smashing itself to atoms before it reached the bottom.

JOSEPH IMBODEN. MRS AUBREY LE BLOND.
ZERMATT, SEPTEMBER, 1896.

CROSSING A SNOW COULOIR (page 73).

Thus with untiring thoroughness Imboden led his little band higher and higher, till at last the summit came in sight and our muscles and overstrained nerves saw rest ahead.

I readily agreed to Imboden's decision that we should go down the ordinary way.

After descending for a considerable distance we stopped, and the guides held a short consultation. It seemed that Roman was anxious to try and fetch the waistcoats and watches and my skirt, and his father did not object.

Wishing him the best of good-luck, we parted by the rocks and trudged on over the snow towards Zermatt. We moved leisurely, as people who climb for pleasure, with no thought of record-breaking; and as it was late in September it was dusk as we neared the village.

Later in the evening I saw Imboden, and asked for news of Roman. He had not arrived, and as time passed we grew uneasy, knowing the speed at which, if alone, he would descend. By 10 P.M. we were really anxious, and great was our relief when a figure with knapsack and ice-axe came swinging up the narrow, cobbled street.

It was an exciting tale he had to tell, though it took a good deal of danger to impress Roman with the notion that there was any at all. Soon after leaving us he came to the first gully. Just as he was about to step into it he heard a rumble. Springing back, he squeezed himself under an overhanging piece of rock, while a huge mass of stones and snow dashed down the mountain, some of the fragments passing right over him—though, thanks to his position, none actually touched him. When tranquility was restored he dashed across to the other side, and immediately after a fresh fall commenced, which lasted for a considerable time. At length he approached without injury the spot he was looking for, far down on the lower slopes, where my skirt had been left, and here he felt that all danger was past. But the extraordinarily dry season had thrown out most people's calculations, and at that very moment he was really in the direst peril. As he ran gaily down the slope of earth and stones a tremendous crash brought him to a standstill, and looking back he saw the smoke of a mighty avalanche of ice coming in a huge wave over the cliffs above. He rushed for shelter, which was near at hand, and from beneath the protection of a great rock he saw the avalanche come on and on with the roar of artillery, and he gazed, fascinated, as it swept majestically past his place of refuge. He could see the mound where lay my skirt with its heap of stones. And now a striking sight met his eyes, for before ever the seething mass could touch it the whole heap rose from the ground and was carried far out of the path of the avalanche, borne along by the violence of the wind which preceded it.

The late John Addington Symonds has related in one of his charming accounts of winter in the Alps that an old woman, sitting peaceably before her châlet door in the sun, was transported by the wind of an avalanche to the top of a lofty pine-tree, where, quite uninjured, she calmly awaited assistance; but that my skirt should have such an adventure brought very strongly home to me the dangers Roman had passed through that afternoon and the escape we had had ourselves.

CHAPTER VIII

LOST IN THE ICE FOR FORTY YEARS

It was in 1786 that the summit of Mont Blanc was reached for the first time. It had been attained on only eleven occasions, and no accidents had happened on it when, in 1820, the catastrophe since known as the Hamel accident, took place.

Dr Joseph Hamel was a Russian savant, and Counsellor of State to the Czar. He much desired to ascend Mont Blanc in order that he might make scientific experiments on the top, and in August 1820, he came to Chamonix for the purpose. It is of no use, and of little interest to general readers, if I enter into particulars of the controversy which this expedition excited. Some declared that Dr Hamel urged his guides to proceed against their better judgment. Others say that the whole party—which included two Englishmen and nine guides—were anxious to continue the ascent, and, indeed, saw no reason for doing otherwise. Certain it is, however that in those days no one was a judge of the condition of snow, and able to tell from its consistency if an avalanche were likely or not.

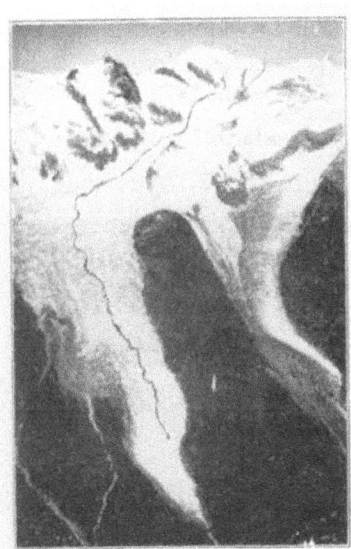

MONT BLANC.

The black line shows the probable course the bodies took during their 40 years' descent in the ice.

By a local Photographer.

Nicolas Winhart, escaping on this occasion with his life, afterwards perished on the Col des Grands Montets in 1875 (page 99).

By a local Photographer.

A Banker at Geneva, who was a most active searcher for Henry Arkwright's body. He was killed in a duel in 1869. It is interesting to compare the old-fashioned costume with that of the present day climber.

By a local Photographer.

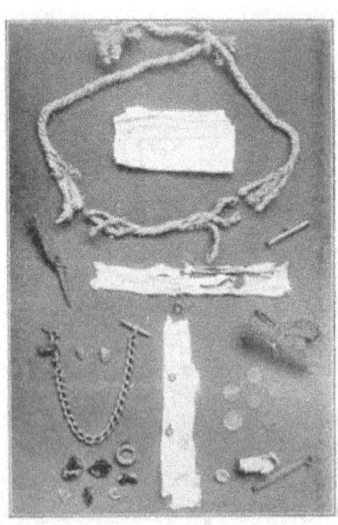

THE RELICS.

The rope was found round the body but worn through in two places by the hip bones. The handkerchief, shirt front with studs, prune stones, watch chain, pencil case, cartridge, spike of alpenstock, coins, glove tied with spare bootlace, etc., all belonged to Henry Arkwright.

The party, which at first numbered fourteen, duly reached the rocks of the Grands Mulets, where it was usual to spend the night. The sky clouded over towards evening, and there was a heavy thunderstorm during the night. Next morning the weather was too unsettled for the ascent to be tried, so a couple of guides were sent down to Chamonix for more provisions, and a second night was spent in camp. Early next morning, in beautiful weather, a start was made, one of the members of the party, Monsieur Selligne, who felt ill, and two guides leaving the others and going down to Chamonix. The rest safely reached the Grand Plateau. The snow, hardened by the night's frost, had thus far supported the weight of the climbers and made their task easy. It was, however, far from consolidated beneath the crust, as the warm wind of the previous days had made it thoroughly rotten.

All were in excellent spirits during the halt for breakfast on the Grand Plateau, that snowy valley which is spread out below the steeper slopes of the final mass of the mountain. Dr Hamel employed part of his time in writing a couple of notes announcing his arrival on the top of Mont Blanc leaving a blank on each to insert the hour. These notes he intended to despatch by carrier pigeon, the bird being with them, imprisoned in a large kettle.

At 10.30 they reached the foot of what is now known as the Ancien Passage. This is a steep snow-slope leading almost directly to the top of Mont Blanc. When the snow is sound, and the ice above does not overhang much, this route is as safe as any other; but a steep slope covered with a layer of rotten snow is always most dangerous. At that time, the Ancien Passage was the only way ever taken up Mont Blanc.

They had ascended a considerable distance, the snow being softer and softer as they rose, and they formed a long line one behind the other, not mounting straight up, but making their way rather across the slope. Six guides walked at the head of the troop, and then, after an interval, the two Englishmen and two more guides, Dr Hamel being last.

All seemed to be going excellently. Everyone plodded along, and rejoiced to be so near the culminating point of the expedition. No thought of danger disturbed them.

Suddenly there was a dull, harsh sound. Immediately the entire surface of the snow began to move. "My God! The avalanche! We are lost!" shrieked the guides. The slope at Dr Hamel's end of the party was not steep,—barely more than 30°—but up above it was more rapid. The leading guides were carried straightway off their feet. Hamel was also swept away by the gathering mass of snow. Using his arms as if swimming, he managed to bring his head to the surface, and as he did so the moving snow slowed down and stopped. In those few moments, some 1200 feet had been descended. At first Dr Hamel thought that he alone had been carried away, but presently he saw his English friends and their guides—no more.

"Where are the others?" cried Dr Hamel. Balmat, who a moment before had let his brother pass on to the head of the party, wrung his hands and answered, "The others are in the crevasse!"

The crevasse! Strange that all had forgotten it! The avalanche had poured into it, filling it to the brim.

"A terrible panic set in. The guides lost all self-control. Some walked about aimlessly, uttering loud cries. Matthieu Balmat sat in sullen silence, rejecting all kind offices with an irritation which made it painful to approach him. Dornford threw himself on the snow in despair, and Henderson, says Hamel, 'was in a condition which made one fear for the consequences.' A few minutes later two other guides extricated themselves, but the remaining three were seen no more. Hamel and Henderson descended into the crevasse, and made every possible attempt to find the lost guides, but without avail; the surviving guides forced them to come out, and sore at heart they returned to Chamonix.

"The three guides who were lost were Pierre Carrier, Pierre Balmat, and Auguste Tairraz. They were the three foremost in the line and felt the first effects of the avalanche. Matthieu Balmat, who was fourth in the line, saved himself by his great personal strength and by presence of mind. Julien Dévouassoud was hurled across the crevasse, and Joseph Marie Couttet was dragged out senseless by his companions, 'nearly black from the weight of snow which had fallen upon him.'"[3]

Scientific men had already begun to give attention to the movement of glaciers. In addition to this, cases had occurred where the remains of persons lost on glaciers had been recovered years afterwards. A travelling seller of hats, crossing the Tschingel Glacier on his way from the Bernese Oberland to Valais, had fallen into a crevasse. Eventually his body and his stock of merchandise was found at the end of the glacier. Near the Grimsel, the remains of a child were discovered in the ice. An old man remembered that many years before a little boy had disappeared in that locality and must doubtless have been lost in a crevasse. These facts were probably known to Dr Hamel, and he made the remark that perhaps in a thousand years, the bodies of his guides might be found. Forbes, who knew more of the subject, believed that, travelling in the ice, they would reach the end of the glacier in forty years.

He was right, for on 15th August 1861, his "bold prediction was verified, and the ice give up its dead." On that day, the guide, Ambrose Simond, who happened to be with some tourists on the lower part of the Glacier des Bossons, discovered some pieces of clothing and human bones. From that time until 1864 the glacier did not cease to render up, piece by piece, the remains and the belongings of the three victims.

An accident, very similar to that which befell Dr Hamel's party, took place in 1866. This has for me a very special interest, as I have met the brother of the Englishman who perished, and have examined all the documents, letters, newspaper cuttings, and photographs relating to the catastrophe. The guide, Sylvain Couttet, an old friend of mine, since dead, has given a moving account of the sad event. Sylvain knew Mont Blanc better than any other native of Chamonix, and though when I knew him he had given up guiding, he desired to add one more ascent of the great white peak to his record, for at that time he had been up ninety-nine times. I accordingly invited him to come with my party when we climbed it from the Italian side. He did so—he had never been up that way before—and I well remember how he slipped himself free of the rope after the last rocks, saying, "Ah, you young people, you go on. The old man will follow." Alone he arrived on the top, strode about over its snowy dome as if to say good-bye, and was just as ready for his work as any of us when, in a stiff gale, we descended the ridge of the Bosses.

But to return to what is known as the Arkwright accident.

In the year 1866, Henry Arkwright, a young man of twenty-nine, aide-de-camp to the Lord-Lieutenant of Ireland, was travelling in Switzerland with his mother and two sisters. Writing from Geneva on 3rd September to a member of his family, he said, "We have ventured to try our luck higher up, as the weather is so warm and settled—as otherwise I should leave Switzerland without seeing a glacier." On what an apparent chance—a run of fine weather—do great issues depend!

The party shortly afterwards moved on to Chamonix, where many excursions were made, thanks to the beautiful weather which still continued. It had now become quite the fashion to go up Mont Blanc, so one is not surprised that Henry Arkwright, though no climber, decided to make the attempt. One of his sisters went with him as far as the hut at the Grands Mulets, and they were accompanied by the guide Michael Simond, and the porters Joseph and François Tournier. Another party proposed also to go up. It consisted of two persons only, Sylvain Couttet and an *employé* of the Hotel Royal named Nicolas Winhart, whom Sylvain had promised to conduct to the top when he had time and opportunity. It was the 12th October when they left Chamonix, and all went well across the crevassed Glacier des Bossons, and they duly reached their night quarters.

While the climbers were absent next day, Miss Fanny Arkwright employed herself with writing and finishing a sketch for her brother.

Meanwhile the two parties, having set out at an early hour, advanced quickly up the snow-slopes. The days were short, and it was desirable to take the most direct route. For years the Ancien Passage had been abandoned, and the more circuitous way by the Corridor used instead. However, the snow was in good order, and as up to then no accidents had happened through falling ice, this danger was little dreaded, though it is sometimes a very real one in the Ancien Passage. So the guides advised that this should be the way chosen, and both parties directed their steps accordingly. Sylvain Couttet has left a remarkable description of the events which followed, and portions of this I now translate from his own words as they appeared in *The Alpine Journal*.

The two parties were together at the beginning of the steep snow-slope. Sylvain's narrative here commences:—"I said to the porter, Joseph Tournier, who had thus far been making the tracks, 'Let us pass on ahead; you have worked long enough. To each of us his share!' It was to this kindly thought for my comrade that, without the slightest doubt, Winhart and I owe our salvation! We had been walking for about ten minutes near some very threatening *séracs* when a crack was heard above us a little to the right. Without reasoning, I instinctively cried, 'Walk quickly!' and I rushed forwards, while someone behind me exclaimed, 'Not in that direction!'

"I heard nothing more; the wind of the avalanche caught me and carried me away in its furious descent. 'Lie down!' I called, and at the same moment I desperately drove my stick into the harder snow beneath, and crouched down on hands and knees, my head bent and turned towards the hurricane. I felt the blocks of ice passing over my back, particles of snow were swept against my face, and I was deafened by a terrible cracking sound like thunder.

"It was only after eight or ten minutes that the air began to clear, and then, always clinging to my axe, I perceived Winhart 6 feet below me, with the point of his stick firmly planted in the ice. The rope by which we were tied to each other was intact. I saw nothing beyond Winhart except the remains of the cloud of snow and a chaos of ice-blocks spread over an area of about 600 feet.

"I called out at the top of my voice—no answer—I became like a madman, I burst out crying, I began to call out again—always the same silence—the silence of death.

"I pulled out my axe, I untied the rope which joined us, and both of us, with what energy remained to us, with our brains on fire and our hearts oppressed with grief, commenced to explore in every direction the enormous mountain of shattered ice-blocks which lay below us. Finally, about 150 feet further down I saw a knapsack—then a man. It was François Tournier, his face terribly mutilated, and his skull smashed in by a piece of ice. The cord had been broken between Tournier and the man next to him. We continued our search in the neighbourhood of his body, but after two hours' work could find nothing more. It was vain to make further efforts! Nothing was visible amongst the masses of *débris*, as big as houses, and we had no tools except my axe and Winhart's stick. We drew the body of poor Tournier after us as far as the Grand Plateau, and with what strength remained to us we descended as fast as we could towards the hut at the Grands Mulets, where a terrible ordeal awaited me—the announcement of the catastrophe to Miss Arkwright.

"The poor child was sitting quietly occupied with her sketching.

"'Well, Sylvain!' she cried on seeing me, 'All has gone well?'

"'Not altogether, Mademoiselle,' I replied, not knowing how to begin.

"Mademoiselle looked at me, noticed my bent head and my eyes full of tears—she rose, came towards me—'What is the matter? Tell me all!'

"I could only answer, 'Have courage, Mademoiselle.'

"She understood me. The brave young girl knelt down and prayed for a few moments, and then got up pale, calm, dry-eyed. 'Now you can tell me everything,' she said, 'I am ready.'

"She insisted on accompanying me at once to Chamonix, where she, in her turn, would have to break the sad tidings to her mother and sister.

"At the foot of the mountain the sister of Mademoiselle met us, happy and smiling.

"Do not ask me any more details of that awful day, I have not the strength to tell them to you."

Thirty-one years passed, when, in 1897, Colonel Arkwright, a brother of Henry Arkwright's, received the following telegram from the Mayor of Chamonix:

"Restes Henry Arkwright peri Mont Blanc 1866 retrouvés."

Once more the glacier had given up its dead, and during these thirty-one years the body of Henry Arkwright had descended 9000 feet in the ice and had been rendered back to his family at the foot of the glacier.

The remains of the Englishman were buried at Chamonix, and perhaps never has so pathetic a service been held there as that which consigned to the earth what was left of him who thirty-one years before had been snatched away in the mighty grip of the avalanche.

Many belongings of the lost one's came by degrees to light. A pocket-handkerchief was intact, and on it as well as on his shirt-front, Henry Arkwright's name and that of his regiment written in marking-ink were legible. Though the shirt was torn to pieces, yet two of the studs and the collar-stud were still in the button-holes and uninjured. The gold pencil-case (I have handled it), opened and shut as smoothly as it had ever done, and on the watch-chain there was not a scratch. A pair of gloves were tied together with a boot-lace which his sister remembered taking from her own boot so that he might have a spare one, and coins, a used cartridge, and various other odds and ends, were all recovered from the ice.

The remains of the guides had been found and brought down soon after the accident, but that of Henry Arkwright had been buried too deeply to be discovered.

In connection with the preservation of bodies in ice the following extract from

The Daily Telegraph for 10th May 1902 is of great interest. It is headed:

MAMMOTH 8000 YEARS OLD

Reuter's representative has had an interview with Mr J. Talbot Clifton, who has lately returned from an expedition in Northern Siberia, undertaken for the purpose of discovering new species of animals.

Mr Clifton gives the following account of the Herz mammoth, which he saw on his arrival at Irkutsk. "It is," he said, "about the size of an elephant, which it resembles somewhat in form. It possesses a trunk, has five toes instead of four, and is a heavy beast. It is supposed to have lived about 8000 years ago. Its age was probably not more than twenty-six years—very young for a mammoth. Its flesh was quite complete, except for a few pieces which had been bitten at by wolves or bears. Most of the hair on the body had been scraped away by ice, but its mane and near foreleg were in perfect preservation and covered with long hair. The hair of the mane was from 4 in. to 5 in. long, and of a yellowish brown colour, while its left leg was covered with black hair. In its stomach was found a quantity of undigested food, and on its tongue was the herbage which it had been eating when it died. This was quite green."

CHAPTER IX

THE MOST TERRIBLE OF ALL ALPINE TRAGEDIES

There is no great mountain in the Alps so easy to ascend as Mont Blanc. There is not one on which there has been such a deplorable loss of life. The very facility with which Mont Blanc can be climbed has tempted hundreds of persons totally unused to and unfitted for mountaineering to go up it, while the tariff for the guides—£4 each—has called into existence a crowd of incapable and inexperienced men who are naturally unable, when the need for it arrives, to face conditions that masters of craft would have avoided by timely retreat.

The great danger of Mont Blanc is its enormous size, and to be lost on its slopes in a snow-storm which may continue for days is an experience few have survived. On a rocky mountain there are landmarks which are of the utmost value in time of fog, but when all is snow and the tracks are obliterated as soon as made, can we wonder if the results have been disastrous when a poorly equipped party has encountered bad weather?

Of all the sad accidents which have happened on Mont Blanc, none exceeds in pathos that in which Messrs Bean, M'Corkindale, Randall, and eight guides perished. None of these gentlemen had any experience of mountaineering. Stimulated rather than deterred by the account given by two climbers who had just come down from the mountain, and had had a narrow escape owing to bad weather, these three men, with their guides, who were "probably about the worst who were then on the Chamonix roll," set out for the Grands Mulets. The weather was doubtful, nevertheless the next morning they started upwards, leaving their only compass at their night quarters.

During the whole of that 6th of September the big telescope at the Châlet of Plan-Praz above Chamonix was fixed on their route, but they could only be seen from time to time, as the mountain was constantly hidden by driving clouds. At last they were observed close to the rocks known as the Petits Mulets not far below the summit. It was then a quarter past two o'clock. There was a terrific wind, and the snow was whirled in clouds. The party could be seen lying down on the ground, to avoid being swept away by the hurricane.

These small figures, in a waste of Snow, may help to give some faint idea of the extent of Alpine Snow-fields.

The Chamonix guide, Sylvain Couttet, had gone to the châlet of Pierre-Pointue, where the riding path ends, to await the return of the climbers. On the morning of the 7th, as there was still no sign of them, Sylvain became uneasy, and mounting to an eminence not far off, from which he could see nearly all the route to the Grands Mulets, he carefully searched for tracks with the aid of his telescope. Snow had fallen during the night, yet there was no trace of footsteps. Seriously alarmed, Sylvain hurried back to Pierre-Pointue, sent a man who was there to Chamonix in order that a search party might be held in readiness, and accompanied by the servant of the little inn he went up the Grands Mulets. Sylvain had arranged that if no one was there he would put out a signal and the search party would then ascend without delay. On reaching the hut at the Grands Mulets his worst fears were realised—it was empty. He now quickly regained Chamonix from where fourteen guides were just starting. He remounted with them immediately. By the time they got a little way above Pierre-Pointue, the snow was again falling heavily, it was impossible to go further. Next day the weather was so bad that the party had to descend to Chamonix, and for several days longer the rain in the valley and the snow on the heights continued.

On the 15th the weather cleared, and Sylvain went up to Plan-Praz to see if from there any traces of the lost ones could be discovered with the telescope. The first glance showed him five black specks near the Petit Mulets, which could be nothing else but the bodies of some of the victims. On the 16th, with twenty-three other guides, Sylvain spent the night at the Grands Mulets. The 17th, they mounted to the spot they had examined with the telescope, and there they found the bodies of Mr M'Corkindale and two porters. Three hundred feet higher was Mr Bean, with his head leaning on his hand, and by him another porter. These were in a perfectly natural position, whereas the others appeared to have slipped to where they were, as their clothes were torn, and the ropes, knapsacks (still containing food), sticks, and so on, lay by the others above.

The five bodies were frozen hard. As complete a search as possible was now made for the remaining six members of the party, but without success. Probably they fell either into a crevasse or down the Italian side of the mountain.

It is no wonder that Mr Mathews calls this "the most lamentable catastrophe ever known in the annals of Alpine adventure."

But the most pathetic part of the story is to come.

During those terrible, hopeless hours Mr Bean had made notes of what was happening, and they tell us all we shall ever know about the disaster:

"Tuesday, 6th September.—I have made the ascent of Mont Blanc with ten persons—eight guides, Mr M'Corkindale, and Mr Randall. We arrived at the summit at half-past two o'clock. Immediately after leaving it I was enveloped in clouds of snow. We passed the night in a grotto excavated out of the snow, affording very uncomfortable shelter, and I was ill all night. *7th September, morning.*—Intense cold—much snow, which falls uninterruptedly. Guides restless. *7th September, evening.*—We have been on Mont Blanc for two days in a terrible snowstorm; we have lost our way, and are in a hole scooped out of the snow at a height of 15,000 feet. I have no hope of descending. Perhaps this book may be found and forwarded. We have no food. My feet are already frozen, and I am exhausted. I have only strength to write a few words. I die in the faith of Jesus Christ, with affectionate thoughts of my family—my remembrance to all. I trust we may meet in heaven."

CHAPTER X

A WONDERFUL SLIDE DOWN A WALL OF ICE

Twice at least in the Alps climbers have lost their footing at the top of a steep slope, and rolled down it for so long a distance that it seemed impossible they could survive. The two plucky mountaineers who have competed in an involuntary race to the bottom of a frozen hillside are Mr Birkbeck, in his famous slide near Mont Blanc, and Mr Whymper, when he made his startling glissade on the Matterhorn.

It was in July 1861 that a party of friends, whose names are well known to all climbers, set out to cross a high glacier pass in the chain of Mont Blanc. The Revs. Leslie Stephen, Charles Hudson, and Messrs Tuckett, Mather, and Birkbeck were the travellers, while in addition to the three magnificent guides, Melchior Anderegg, Perren, and Bennen, there were two local guides from the village of St Gervais.

Let me give the account of the accident in Mr Hudson's own words. How sad to think that, only four years later, this capable and brave mountaineer himself perished on the grim north slopes of the Matterhorn!

The Col de Miage is reached by a steep slope of ice or frozen snow, and is just a gap in the chain of peaks which runs south-west from Mont Blanc. Col is the word used for a pass in French-speaking districts.

"On the morning of the 11th, at 3.30, we left the friendly rock on or near which we had passed the night, and at 7 o'clock we had reached the summit of the Col de Miage. Here we sat down on a smooth, hard plain of snow, and had our second breakfast. Shortly afterwards Birkbeck had occasion to leave us for a few minutes, though his departure was not remarked at the time. When we discovered his absence, Melchior followed his footsteps, and I went after him, and, to our dismay, we saw the tracks led to the edge of the ice-slope, and then suddenly stopped. The conclusion was patent at a glance. I was fastening two ropes together, and Melchior had already bound one end round his chest, with a view to approach or even descend a portion of the slope for a better view, when some of the party descried Birkbeck a long way below us. He had fallen an immense distance.

"My first impulse led me to wish that Melchior and I should go down to Birkbeck as fast as possible, and leave the rest to follow with the ropes; but on proposing this plan some of the party objected. For a considerable time Birkbeck shouted to us, not knowing whether we could see his position. His course had been arrested at a considerable distance above the bottom of the slope, by what means we know not; and just below him stretched a snow-covered crevasse, across which he must pass if he went further. We shouted to him to remain where he was, but no distinguishable sounds reached him; and to our dismay we presently saw him gradually moving downwards—then he stopped—again he moved forwards and again—he was on the brink of the crevasse; but we could do nothing for him. At length he slipped down upon the slope of snow which bridged the abyss. I looked anxiously to see if it would support his weight, and, to my relief, a small black speck continued visible. This removed my immediate cause of apprehension, and after a time he moved clear of this frail support down to the point where we afterwards joined him. Bennen was first in the line, and after we had descended some distance he untied himself and went down to Birkbeck. It was 9.30 when we reached him. He told us he was becoming faint and suffering from cold. On hearing this, Melchoir and I determined to delay no longer, and, accordingly, unroped and trotted down to the point where we could descend from the rocks to the slope upon which he was lying. Arrived at the place, I sat on the snow, and let Birkbeck lean against me, while I asked him if he felt any internal injury or if his ribs pained him. His manner of answering gave me strong grounds for hoping that there was little to fear on that score."

Mr Hudson gives a graphic description of poor Mr Birkbeck's appearance when he was found on the snow. "His legs, thighs, and the lower part of his body were quite naked, with his trousers down about his feet. By his passage over the snow, the skin was removed from the outside of the legs and thighs, the knees, and the whole of the lower part of the back, and part of the ribs, together with some from the nose and forehead. He had not lost much blood, but he presented a most ghastly spectacle of bloody raw flesh. This, added to his great prostration, and our consciousness of the distance and difficulties which separated him from any bed, rendered the sight most trying. He never lost consciousness. He afterwards described his descent as one of extreme rapidity, too fast to allow of his realising the sentiment of fear, but not sufficiently so to deprive him of thought. Sometimes he descended feet first, sometimes head first, then he went sideways, and once or twice he had the sensation of shooting through the air.

"The slope where he first lost his footing was gentle, and he tried to stop himself with his fingers and nails, but the snow was too hard. He had no fear during the descent, owing to the extreme rapidity; but when he came to a halt on the snow, and was ignorant as to whether we saw, or could reach him, he experienced deep anguish of mind in the prospect of a lingering death. Happily, however, the true Christian principles in which he had been brought up, led him to cast himself upon the protection of that merciful Being who alone could help him. His prayers were heard, and immediately answered by the removal of his fears."

The account of how the injured man was brought down to the valley is very exciting. Mr Hudson continues:—"The next thing was to get him down as fast as possible, and the sledge suggested itself as the most feasible plan. Only the day before, at Contamines, I had had the boards made for it, and without them the runners (which, tied together, served me as an alpenstock) would have been useless. Two or three attempts were made before I could get the screws to fit the holes in the boards and runners, and poor Melchior, who was watching me, began to show signs of despair. At length the operation was completed, and the sledge was ready. We spread a plaid, coats, and flannel shirts over the boards, then laid Birkbeck at full length on them, and covered him as well as we could.

"Now came the 'tug-of-war,' for the snow was much softened by the sun, the slope was steep, and there were several crevasses ahead; added to this, there was difficulty in getting good hold of the sledge, and every five or six steps one of the bearers plunged so deeply in the snow that we were obliged to halt. Birkbeck was all the time shivering so much that the sledge was sensibly shaken, and all the covering we could give him was but of little use.

"I was well aware of the great danger Birkbeck was in, owing to the vast amount of skin which was destroyed, and I felt that every quarter of an hour saved was of very great importance; still the frequent delay could not be avoided."

So matters continued till the party was clear of the glacier. Then Mr Tuckett went ahead to Chamonix, a ten hours' tramp or so, in search of an English doctor, and on the way left orders for a carriage to be sent as far as there was a driving road, to meet the wounded man, and more men beyond to help in carrying him. The chief part of the transport was done by the three great guides, Melchoir, Bennen, and Perren, and was often over "abrupt slopes of rock, which to an ordinary walker would have appeared difficult, even without anything to carry. We had so secured Birkbeck with ropes and straps, that he could not slip off the sledge, otherwise he would on these occasions at once have parted company with his stretcher, and rolled down the rocks."

At last, after incredible toil, they reached the pastures, and at about three o'clock in the afternoon eight hours after the accident, they got to the home of one of the guides, where they were able to make poor Mr Birkbeck more comfortable before undertaking the rest of the journey, warming his feet and wrapping him in blankets. For two hours more the poor fellow had to be carried down, and then they met the carriage, in which he was driven to St Gervais, accompanied by the doctor from Chamonix.

Thanks to the skilful treatment and excellent nursing he received, Mr Birkbeck made a good recovery, though, of course, it was weeks before he could leave his bed.

Mr Hudson ends his wonderfully interesting narrative with an account of a visit he paid later in the season to the place where the accident happened. He says "The result of our observations is as follows: 'The height of the Col de Miage is 11,095. The height of the point at which Birkbeck finally came to a standstill is 9328 feet; so the distance he fell is, in *perpendicular* height, 1767 feet." As part of the slope would be at a gentle angle, one may believe that the slip was over something like a mile of surface! Mr Hudson continues:
—"During the intervening three weeks, vast changes had taken place in the glacier. The snowy coating had left the couloir in parts, thus exposing ice in the line of Birkbeck's course, as well as a rock mid-way in the slope, against which our poor friend would most likely have struck, had the accident happened later.

"This is one of that long chain of providential arrangements, by the combination of which we were enabled to save Birkbeck's life.

(1) The recent snow, and favourable state of the glacier, enabled us to take an easier and much quicker route, if not the only one possible for a wounded man.
(2) We had a singularly strong party of guides, without which we could not have got him down in time to afford any chance of his recovery.
(3) If we had not had real efficient men as travellers in the party we should not have got the telegram sent to Geneva; and a few hours' delay in the arrival of Dr Metcalfe would probably have been fatal.
(4) The day was perfectly calm and cloudless; had there been wind or absence of sun, the cold might have been too much for such a shaken system to bear.
(5) We had with us the very unusual addition of a sledge, without which it would have been scarcely possible to have carried him down.

"One thing there was which greatly lessened the mental trial to those engaged in bringing Birkbeck down to St Gervais, and afterwards in attending upon him, and that was, his perfect calmness and patience—and of these I cannot speak too highly. No doubt it contributed greatly to his recovery."

CHAPTER XI

AN ADVENTURE ON THE TRIFT PASS

Few passes leading out of the Valley of Zermatt are oftener crossed than the Trift. It is not considered a difficult pass, but the rocks on the Zinal side are loose and broken and the risk of falling stones is great at certain hours in the day. The Zinal side of the Trift is in shadow in the early morning, and therefore most climbers will either make so early a start from the Zermatt side that they can be sure of descending the dangerous part before the sun has thawed the icy fetters which hold the stones together during the night, or else they will set out from the Zinal side, and sleep at a little inn on a patch of rocks which jut out from the glacier at the foot of the pass, from which the top of the Trift can be reached long before there is any risk from a cannonade.

One of the earliest explorers of this pass, however, Mr Thomas W. Hinchliff, neglected the precaution of a sufficiently early start, and his party very nearly came to grief in consequence.

He has given us an excellent description in *Peaks, Passes, and Glaciers* of what befell after they had got over the great difficulties, as they seemed in those days, of descending the steep wall of rock on the Zinal side. I will now begin to quote from his article:

"Being thoroughly tired of the rocks, we resolved as soon as possible to get upon the ice where it swept the base of the precipices. The surface, however, was furrowed by parallel channels of various magnitudes; some several feet in depth, formed originally by the descent of stones and avalanches from the heights; and we found one of these troughlike furrows skirting the base of the rocks we stood upon. One by one we entered, flattering ourselves that the covering of snow would afford us pretty good footing, but this soon failed; the hard blue ice showed on the surface, and we found ourselves rather in a difficulty, for the sides of our furrow were higher here than at the point where we entered it, and so overhanging that it was impossible to get out.

"Delay was dangerous, for the *débris* far below warned us that at any moment a shower of stones might come flying down our channel; a glissade was equally dangerous; for, though we might have shot down safely at an immense speed for some hundreds of feet, we should finally have been dashed into a sea of crevasses. Cachat in front solved the puzzle, and showed us how, by straddling with the feet as far apart as possible, the heel of each foot could find pretty firm hold in a mixture of half snow and half ice, his broad back, like a solid rock, being ready to check any slip of those behind him.

"We were soon safe upon a fine open plateau of the *névé*, where we threaded our way among a few snow crevasses requiring caution, and then prepared for a comfortable halt in an apparently safe place.

"The provision knapsacks were emptied and used as seats; bottles of red wine were stuck upright in the snow; a goodly leg of cold mutton on its sheet of paper formed the centre, garnished with hard eggs and bread and cheese, round which we ranged ourselves in a circle. High festival was held under the deep blue heavens, and now and then, as we looked up at the wonderful wall of rocks which we had descended, we congratulated ourselves on the victory. M. Seiler's oranges supplied the rare luxury of a dessert, and we were just in the full enjoyment of the delicacy when a booming sound, like the discharge of a gun far over our heads, made us all at once glance upwards to the top of the Trifthorn. Close to its craggy summit hung a cloud of dust, like dirty smoke, and in few seconds another and a larger one burst forth several hundred feet lower. A glance through the telescope showed that a fall of rocks had commenced, and the fragments were leaping down from ledge to ledge in a series of cascades. The uproar became tremendous; thousands of fragments making every variety of noise according to their size, and producing the effect of a fire of musketry and artillery combined, thundered downwards from so great a height that we waited anxiously for some considerable time to see them reach the snow-field below. As nearly as we could estimate the distance, we were 500 yards from the base of the rocks, so we thought that, come what might, we were in a tolerably secure position. At last we saw many of the blocks plunge into the snow after taking their last fearful leap; presently much larger fragments followed; the noise grew fiercer and fiercer, and huge blocks began to fall so near to us that we jumped to our feet, preparing to dodge them to the best of our ability. 'Look out!' cried someone, and we opened out right and left at the approach of a monster, evidently weighing many hundredweights, which was coming right at us like a huge shell fired from a mortar. It fell with a heavy thud not more than 20 feet from us, scattering lumps of snow into the circle."

Years afterwards a very sad accident occurred at this spot, a lady being struck and killed by a falling stone. In this case the fatality was unquestionably due to the start having been made at too late an hour. An inn in the Trift Valley makes it easy to reach the pass soon after dawn.

THE PERILS OF THE MOMING PASS.

In 1864 many peaks remained unsealed, and passes untraversed in the Zermatt district, though now almost every inch of every mountain has felt the foot of man. Yet even now few passes have been made there so difficult and dangerous (if Mr Whymper's route be exactly followed) as that of the Moming, from Zinal to Zermatt. Mr Whymper gives a most graphic and exciting description of what befell his party, which included Mr Moore and the two famous guides Almer and Croz. Having slept at some filthy châlets, the climbers, first passing over easy mountain slopes, gained a level glacier. Beyond this a way towards the unexplored gap in the ridge, which they called the Moming Pass, had to be decided on. The choice lay between difficult and perhaps impassable rocks, and an ice-slope so steep and broken that it appeared likely to turn out impracticable. In fact it was the sort of position that whichever route was chosen the climbers were sure, when once on it, to wish it had been the other. Finally, the ice-slope, over which a line of ice-cliffs hung threateningly, lurching right above the track to be taken, was decided on, and the whole party advanced for the attack. Mr Whymper writes:

"Across this ice-slope Croz now proceeded to cut. It was executing a flank movement in the face of an enemy by whom we might be attacked at any moment. The peril was obvious. It was a monstrous folly. It was foolhardiness. A retreat should have been sounded.[4]

"'I am not ashamed to confess,' wrote Moore in his Journal, 'that during the whole time we were crossing this slope my heart was in my mouth, and I never felt relieved from such a load of care as when, after, I suppose, a passage of about twenty minutes, we got on to the rocks and were in safety.... I have never heard a positive oath come from Almer's mouth, but the language in which he kept up a running commentary, more to himself than to me, as we went along, was stronger than I should have given him credit for using. His prominent feeling seemed to be one of *indignation* that we should be in such a position, and self-reproach at being a party to the proceeding; while the emphatic way in which, at intervals, he exclaimed, 'Quick; be quick,' sufficiently betokened his alarm.

"It was not necessary to admonish Croz to be quick. He was fully as alive to the risk as any of the others. He told me afterwards that this place was the most dangerous he had ever crossed, and that no consideration whatever would tempt him to cross it again. Manfully did he exert himself to escape from the impending destruction. His head, bent down to his work, never turned to the right or to the left. One, two, three, went his axe, and then he stepped on to the spot he had been cutting. How painfully insecure should we have considered those steps at any other time! But now, we thought only of the rocks in front, and of the hideous *séracs*, lurching over above us, apparently in the act of falling.

"We got to the rocks in safety, and if they had been doubly as difficult as they were, we should still have been well content. We sat down and refreshed the inner man, keeping our eyes on the towering pinnacles of ice under which we had passed, but which, now, were almost beneath us. Without a preliminary warning sound, one of the largest—as high as the Monument at London Bridge—fell upon the slope below. The stately mass heeled over as if upon a hinge (holding together until it bent thirty degrees forwards), then it crushed out its base, and, rent into a thousand fragments, plunged vertically down upon the slope that we had crossed! Every atom of our track that was in its course was obliterated; all the new snow was swept away, and a broad sheet of smooth, glassy ice, showed the resistless force with which it had fallen.

"It was inexcusable to follow such a perilous path, but it is easy to understand why it was taken. To have retreated from the place where Croz suggested a change of plan, to have descended below the reach of danger, and to have mounted again by the route which Almer suggested, would have been equivalent to abandoning the excursion; for no one would have passed another night in the châlet on the Arpitetta Alp. 'Many' says Thucydides, 'though seeing well the perils ahead, are forced along by fear of dishonour—as the world calls it—so that, vanquished by a mere word, they fall into irremediable calamities.' Such was nearly the case here. No one could say a word in justification of the course which was adopted; all were alive to the danger that was being encountered; yet a grave risk was deliberately—although unwillingly—incurred, in preference to admitting, by withdrawal from an untenable position, that an error of judgment had been committed.

"After a laborious trudge over many species of snow, and through many varieties of vapour—from the quality of a Scotch mist to that of a London fog—we at length stood on the depression between the Rothhorn and the Schallhorn.[5] A steep wall of snow was upon the Zinal side of the summit; but what the descent was like on the other side we could not tell, for a billow of snow tossed over its crest by the western winds, suspended o'er Zermatt with motion arrested, resembling an ocean-wave frozen in the act of breaking, cut off the view.[6]

"Croz—held hard in by the others, who kept down the Zinal side—opened his shoulders, flogged down the foam, and cut away the cornice to its junction with the summit; then boldly leaped down and called on us to follow him.

"It was well for us now that we had such a man as leader. An inferior or less daring guide would have hesitated to enter upon the descent in a dense mist; and Croz himself would have done right to pause had he been less magnificent in *physique*. He acted, rather than said, 'Where snow lies fast, there man can go; where ice exists, a way may be cut; it is a question of power; I have the power—all you have to do is to follow me.' Truly, he did not spare himself, and could he have performed the feats upon the boards of a theatre that he did upon this occasion, he would have brought down the house with thunders of applause. Here is what Moore wrote in *his* Journal "('The descent bore a strong resemblance to the Col de Pilatte, but was very much steeper and altogether more difficult, which is saying a good deal. Croz was in his element, and selected his way with marvellous sagacity, while Almer had an equally honourable and, perhaps, more responsible post in the rear, which he kept with his usual steadiness.... One particular passage has impressed itself on my mind as one of the most nervous I have ever made. We had to pass along a crest of ice, a mere knife-edge,—on our left a broad crevasse, whose bottom was lost in blue haze, and on our right, at an angle of 70°, or more, a slope falling to a similar gulf below. Croz, as he went along the edge, chipped small notches in the ice, in which we placed our feet, with the toes well turned out, doing all we knew to preserve our balance. While stepping from one of these precarious footholds to another, I staggered for a moment. I had not really lost my footing; but the agonised tone in which Almer, who was behind me, on seeing me waver, exclaimed, "Slip not, sir!" gave us an even livelier impression than we already had of the insecurity of the position.... One huge chasm, whose upper edge was far above the lower one, could neither be leaped nor turned, and threatened to prove an insuperable barrier. But Croz showed himself equal to the emergency. Held up by the rest of the party, he cut a series of holes for the hands and feet down and along the almost perpendicular wall of ice forming the upper side of the *schrund*. Down this slippery staircase we crept, with our faces to the wall, until a point was reached where the width of the chasm was not too great for us to drop across. Before we had done, we got quite accustomed to taking flying leaps over the *schrunds*.... To make a long story short; after a most desperate and exciting struggle, and as bad a piece of ice-work as it is possible to imagine, we emerged on to the upper plateau of the Hohlicht Glacier.')"

From here, in spite of many further difficulties necessitating a long *detour*, the party safely descended to Zermatt by the familiar Trift path.

CHAPTER XII

AN EXCITING PASSAGE OF THE COL DE PILATTE

Even now the valleys and mountains of Dauphiné are neglected in comparison with the ranges of Mont Blanc, Monte Rosa, and other famous mountain chains of the Alps. In 1864, when Mr Whymper with his friends Messrs Moore and Walker undertook a summer campaign there, it was practically unexplored from the climbers' point of view. The party was a skilful and experienced one, the guides, Almer and Croz, of the highest class, and the *esprit de corps* in the little army of invasion most admirable. Thus it is no wonder that peak after peak fell before them, passes were accomplished at the first assault, and no accident or annoyance spoilt the splendid series of expeditions which were so successfully accomplished. Of these I have taken the account of the crossing of the Col de Pilatte, a high glacier pass, for, though it was excelled in difficulty by other climbs, yet it is so wittily described by Mr Whymper in his *Scrambles in the Alps*, and gives so excellent an idea of the sort of work met with on glaciers, and the ease with which a thoroughly competent party tackles it, that it cannot fail to be read with interest.

The three Englishmen had been joined by a French friend of theirs, Monsieur Reynaud, and had left their night quarters at Entraigues at 3.30 A.M. on the morning of 27th June. Their course was prodigiously steep. *In less than two miles difference of latitude they rose one mile of absolute height.* The route, however, was not really difficult, and they made good progress. They had reached the foot of the steep part when I take up the narrative in Mr Whymper's own words:

"At 9.30 A.M. we commenced the ascent of the couloir leading from the nameless glacier to a point in the ridge, just to the east of Mont Bans.[7] So far the route had been nothing more than a steep grind in an angle where little could be seen, but now views opened out in several directions, and the way began to be interesting. It was more so, perhaps, to us than to our companion M. Reynaud, who had no rest in the last night. He was, moreover, heavily laden. Science was to be regarded—his pockets were stuffed with books; heights and angles were to be observed—his knapsack was filled with instruments; hunger was to be guarded against—his shoulders were ornamented with a huge nimbus of bread, and a leg of mutton swung behind from his knapsack, looking like an overgrown tail. Like a good-hearted fellow he had brought this food thinking we might be in need of it. As it happened, we were well provided for, and, having our own packs to carry, could not relieve him of his superfluous burdens, which, naturally, he did not like to throw away. As the angles steepened, the strain on his strength became more and more apparent. At last he began to groan. At first a most gentle and mellow groan; and as we rose so did his groans, till at last the cliffs were groaning in echo, and we were moved to laughter.

START OF A CLIMBING PARTY BY MOONLIGHT.

SHADOWS AT SUNRISE.

A STANDING GLISSADE.

AN EASY DESCENT.

"Croz cut the way with unflagging energy throughout the whole of the ascent, and at 10.45 we stood on the summit of our pass, intending to refresh ourselves with a good halt; but just at that moment a mist, which had been playing about the ridge, swooped down and blotted out the whole of the view on the northern side. Croz was the only one who caught a glimpse of the descent, and it was deemed advisable to push on immediately, while its recollection was fresh in his memory. We are consequently unable to tell anything about the summit of the pass, except that it lies immediately to the east of Mont Bans, and is elevated about 11,300 feet above the level of the sea. It is one of the highest passes in Dauphiné. We called it the Col de Pilatte.

"We commenced to descend towards the Glacier de Pilatte by a slope of smooth ice, the face of which, according to the measurement of Mr Moore, had an inclination of 54°! Croz still led, and the others followed at intervals of about 15 feet, all being tied together, and Almer occupying the responsible position of last man: the two guides were therefore about 70 feet apart. They were quite invisible to each other from the mist, and looked spectral even to us. But the strong man could be heard by all hewing out the steps below, while every now and then the voice of the steady man pierced the cloud: 'Slip not, dear sirs; place well your feet; stir not until you are certain.'

"For three-quarters of an hour we progressed in this fashion. The axe of Croz all at once stopped. 'What is the matter, Croz?' 'Bergschrund, gentlemen.' 'Can we get over?' 'Upon my word, I don't know; I think we must jump.' The clouds rolled away right and left as he spoke. The effect was dramatic! It was a *coup de théâtre*, preparatory to the 'great sensation leap' which was about to be executed by the entire company.

"Some unseen cause, some cliff or obstruction in the rocks underneath, had caused our wall of ice to split into two portions, and the huge fissure which had thus been formed extended, on each hand, as far as could be seen. We, on the slope above, were separated from the slope below by a mighty crevasse. No running up and down to look for an easier place to cross could be done on an ice-slope of 54°; the chasm had to be passed then and there.

"A downward jump of 15 or 16 feet, and a forward leap of 7 or 8 feet had to be made at the same time. That is not much, you will say. It was not much. It was not the quantity, but it was the quality of the jump which gave to it its particular flavour. You had to hit a narrow ridge of ice. If that was passed, it seemed as if you might roll down for ever and ever. If it was not attained, you dropped into the crevasse below, which, although partly choked by icicles and snow that had fallen from above, was still gaping in many places, ready to receive an erratic body.

"Croz untied Walker in order to get rope enough, and warning us to hold fast, sprang over the chasm. He alighted cleverly on his feet; untied himself and sent up the rope to Walker, who followed his example. It was then my turn, and I advanced to the edge of the ice. The second which followed was what is called a supreme moment. That is to say, I felt supremely ridiculous. The world seemed to revolve at a frightful pace, and my stomach to fly away. The next moment I found myself sprawling in the snow, and then, of course, vowed that it was nothing, and prepared to encourage my friend Reynaud.

"He came to the edge and made declarations. I do not believe that he was a whit more reluctant to pass the place than we others, but he was infinitely more demonstrative—in a word, he was French. He wrung his hands, 'Oh! what a *diable* of a place!' 'It is nothing, Reynaud,' I said, 'it is nothing.' 'Jump,' cried the others, 'jump.' But he turned round, as far as one can do such a thing in an ice-step, and covered his face with his hands, ejaculating, 'Upon my word, it is not possible. No! no! no! it is not possible.'

"How he came over I scarcely know. We saw a toe—it seemed to belong to Moore; we saw Reynaud a flying body, coming down as if taking a header into water; with arms and legs all abroad, his leg of mutton flying in the air, his bâton escaped from his grasp; and then we heard a thud as if a bundle of carpets had been pitched out of a window. When set upon his feet he was a sorry spectacle; his head was a great snowball; brandy was trickling out of one side of the knapsack, chartreuse out of the other—we bemoaned its loss, but we roared with laughter.

"I cannot close this chapter without paying tribute to the ability with which Croz led us, through a dense mist, down the remainder of the Glacier de Pilatte. As an exhibition of strength and skill, it has seldom been surpassed in the Alps or elsewhere. On this almost unknown and very steep glacier, he was perfectly at home, even in the mists. Never able to see 50 feet ahead, he still went on with the utmost certainty, and without having to retrace a single step; and displayed from first to last consummate knowledge of the materials with which he was dealing. Now he cut steps down one side of a *sérac*, went with a dash at the other side, and hauled us up after him; then cut away along a ridge until a point was gained from which we could jump on to another ridge; then, doubling back, found a snow-bridge, over which he crawled on hands and knees, towed us across by the legs, ridiculing our apprehensions, mimicking our awkwardness, declining all help, bidding us only to follow him.

"About 1 P.M. we emerged from the mist and found ourselves just arrived upon the level portion of the glacier, having, as Reynaud properly remarked, come down as quickly as if there had not been any mist at all. Then we attacked the leg of mutton which my friend had so thoughtfully brought with him, and afterwards raced down, with renewed energy, to La Bérarde."

CHAPTER XIII

AN ADVENTURE ON THE ALETSCH GLACIER

Mr William Longman, a former Vice-President of the Alpine Club, has given us an interesting account in *The Alpine Journal* of an exciting adventure which happened to his son in August 1862.

The party, consisting of Mr Longman, his son, aged fifteen, two friends, two guides, and a porter, set out one lovely morning from the Eggischhorn Hotel for an excursion on the Great Aletsch Glacier. The names of the guides were Fedier and Andreas Weissenflüh.

Mr Longman writes:—"We started in high spirits; the glacier was in perfect order; no fresh snow covered the ice; the crevasses were all unhidden; and no one thought it necessary to use the rope. I felt it to be a wise precaution, however, to place my son, a boy of fifteen years of age, under the care of the Eggischhorn porter. It was his second visit to Switzerland, and he could, I am sure, have taken good care of himself, but I felt it was my duty to place him under the care of a guide. I have no wish to throw undeserved blame on the guide; but his carelessness was unquestionably the cause of the accident. He began wrong, and I ought to have interfered. He tied his handkerchief in a knot, and, holding it himself, gave it to my son to hold also in his hand. This was worse than useless, and, in fact, was the cause of danger, for it partly deprived him of that free and active use of his limbs which is essential to safety. It threw him off his guard. Except at a crevasse, it was unnecessary for the boy to have anything to hold by; and, at a crevasse, the handkerchief would have been insufficient. The impression that there was no real danger, and that all that was required was caution in crossing the crevasses, prevented my interfering. So the guide went on, his hand holding the handkerchief behind him, and my son following, his hand also holding the handkerchief. Many a time I complained to the guide that he took my boy over wide parts of the crevasses because he would not trouble himself to diverge from his path, and many a time did I compel him to turn aside to a narrower chasm. At last, I was walking a few yards to his left, and had stepped over a narrow crevasse, when I was startled by an exclamation. I turned round suddenly, and my son was out of sight! I will not harrow up my own feelings, or those of my readers, by attempting to describe the frightful anguish that struck me to the heart; but will only relate, plainly and calmly, all that took place. When my son fell, the crevasse, which I had crossed so easily, became wider, and its two sides were joined by a narrow ridge of ice. It was obviously impossible to ascertain exactly what had taken place; but I am convinced that the guide went on in his usual thoughtless way, with his hand behind him, drawing my son after him, and that, as soon as he placed his foot on the narrow ridge, he slipped and fell. I rushed to the edge of the crevasse and called out to my poor boy. To my inexpressible delight he at once answered me calmly and plainly. As I afterwards ascertained, he was 50 feet from me, and neither could he see us nor we see him. But he was evidently unhurt; he was not frightened, and he was not beyond reach. In an instant Weissenflüh was ready to descend into the crevasse. He buckled on one of my belts,[8] fixed it to the rope, and told us to lower him down. My two friends and I, and the other two guides, held on to the rope, and slowly and gradually, according to Weissenflüh's directions, we paid it out. It was a slow business, but we kept on encouraging my son, and receiving cheery answers from him in return. At last Weissenflüh told us, to our intense joy, that he had reached my son, that he had hold of him, and that we might haul up. Strongly and steadily we held on, drawing both the boy and the guide, as we believed, nearer and nearer, till at length, to our inexpressible horror, we drew up Weissenflüh alone. He had held my son by the collar of his coat. The cloth was wet, his hand was cold, and the coat slipped from his grasp. I was told that when my boy thus again fell he uttered a cry, but either I heard it not or forgot it. The anguish of the moment prevented my noticing it, and, fortunately, we none of us lost our presence of mind, but steadily held on to the rope. Poor Weissenflüh reached the surface exhausted, dispirited, overwhelmed with grief. He threw himself on the glacier in terrible agony. In an instant Fedier was ready to descend, and we began to lower him; but the crevasse was narrow, and Fedier could not squeeze himself through the ice. We had to pull him up again before he had descended many feet. By this time the brave young Weissenflüh had recovered, and was ready again to go down. But we thought it desirable to take the additional precaution of lowering the other rope, with one of the belts securely fixed to it. My son quickly got hold of it, and placed the belt round his body, but he told us his hands were too cold to buckle it. Weissenflüh now again descended, and soon he told us he had fixed the belt. With joyful heart some hauled away at one rope and some at the other, till at length, after my son had been buried in the ice for nearly half an hour, both he and the guide were brought to the surface.... Let a veil rest over the happiness of meeting. My boy's own account of what befell him is, that he first fell sideways on to a ledge in the crevasse, and then vertically, but providentially with his feet downwards, till his progress was arrested by the narrowness of the crevasse. He says he is sure he was stopped by being wedged in, because his feet were hanging loose. His arms were free. He believes the distance he fell, when Weissenflüh dropped him, was about three or four yards, and that he fell to nearly, but not quite, the same place as that to which he fell at first, and that, in his first position, he could not have put the belt on. His fall was evidently a slide for the greater part of the distance; had it been a sheer fall it would have been impossible to escape severe injury."

A LOYAL COMPANION

The following is taken from *The Times* of 23rd July 1886.

"On Tuesday, 13th July, Herr F. Burckhardt, member of the Basel section of the Swiss Alpine Club, accompanied by the guides Fritz Teutschmann and Johann Jossi, both from Grindelwald, made an attempt to ascend the Jungfrau from the side of the Little Scheideck. After leaving the Guggi cabin the party mounted the glacier of the same name. The usual precautions were of course taken—that is to say, the three men were roped together, Herr Burckhardt in the middle, one of the guides before, the other behind him. When the climbers reached the *séracs*, at a point marked on the Siegfried Karte as being at an elevation of 2700 mètres, an enormous piece of ice broke off from the upper part of the glacier, and came thundering down. Although by good fortune the mass of the avalanche did not sweep across the path of the three men, they were struck by several large blocks of ice, and sent flying. Jossi, who was leading, went head first into a crevasse of unfathomable depth, dragging after him Herr Burckhardt, who, however, contrived to hold on to the edge of the crevasse, but in such a position that he could not budge, and was unable to help either himself or Jossi. Their lives at that moment depended absolutely on the staunchness of Teutschmann, who alone had succeeded in keeping his feet. It was beyond his power to do more; impossible by his own unaided strength to haul up the two men who hung by the rope. If he had given way a single step all three would have been precipitated to the bottom of the crevasse. So there he stood, with feet and ice-axe firmly planted, holding on for dear life, conscious that the end was a mere question of time, and a very short time; his strength was rapidly waning, and then? It would have been easy for the two to escape by sacrificing the third. One slash of Burckhardt's knife would have freed both Teutschmann and himself. But no such dastardly idea occurred to either of them. They were resolved to live or die together. Half an hour passed; they had almost abandoned hope, and Teutschmann's forces were well-nigh spent, when help came just in time to save them. The same morning another party, consisting of two German tourists, and the two guides Peter Schlegel and Rudolph Kaufmann, had started from the Little Scheideck for the Jungfrau, and coming on traces of Burckhardt's party had followed them up, and arrived before it was too late on the scene of the accident. Without wasting a moment Schlegel went down into the crevasse and fastened Jossi to another rope, so that those above were enabled to draw him up and release Burckhardt and Teutschmann. Jossi, although bruised and exhausted, was able to walk to the Scheideck, and all reached Grindelwald in safety."

On a Snow-covered Glacier.

The party is crossing a Snow Bridge, and the rope between the centre and last man is too slack for safety.

When it is remembered how few people make this expedition, the escape of Mr Burckhardt's party is the more wonderful, and would not have been possible unless other climbers had taken the same route that day. This way up the Jungfrau is always somewhat exposed to falling ice, though sometimes it is less dangerous than at other times. As the editor of *The Alpine Journal* has written, "no amount of experience can avail against falling missiles, and the best skill of the mountaineer is shown in keeping out of their way."

A BRAVE GUIDE

The brave actions of guides are so many in number that it would be impossible to tell of them all, and many noble deeds have never found their way into print. The following, however, is related of a guide with whom I have made many ascents, and is furthermore referred to in *The Alpine Journal* as "an act of bravery for which it would be hard to find a parallel in the annals of mountaineering."

On 1st September 1898, a party of two German gentlemen with a couple of guides went up Piz Palü, a glacier-clad peak frequently ascended from

Pontresina. One of the guides was a Tyrolese, Klimmer by name, the other a native of the Engadine, Schnitzler.

They had completed the ascent of the actual peak, and were on their way down, some distance below the Bellavista Saddle. Here there are several large crevasses, and the slope is very steep at this point. I remember passing down it with Schnitzler the previous January, and finding much care needed to cross a big chasm. Schnitzler was leading, then came the two travellers, finally the Tyrolese, who came down last man. Suddenly Schnitzler, who must have stepped on a snow-bridge, and Herr Nasse dropped without a sound into the chasm. Dr Borchardt was dragged some steps after them, but managed to check himself on the very brink of the abyss. Behind was Klimmer, but on so steep a surface that he could give no help beyond standing firm. At last, after some anxious moments, came a call from below, "Pull!" They did their best but in vain. "My God!" cried Schnitzler from below, "I can't get out!" A period of terrible apprehension followed. Herr Nasse was entreated to try and help a little, or to cut himself free from the rope, as he appeared to be suffering greatly. But he was helpless, hanging with the rope pressing his chest till he could hardly breathe, and cried out that he could stand it no longer. Dr Borchardt made a plucky attempt to render assistance, and the desperate endeavour nearly caused him to fall also into the crevasse.

Martin Schocher standing, Schnitzler sitting. On the Summit of Crast'Agüzza in Mid-Winter.

A projecting Cornice of Snow, which might fall at any moment. The accident on the Lyskamm, described on page 35, was due to the breaking of a Cornice.

Between Earth and Sky (page 163).

An extremely narrow Snow Ridge, but a much easier one to pass than that described by Mr Moore
(page 160)

The position was terrible, and Herr Nasse was at the end of his forces. He called out in a dying voice that he could bear no more—it was the last time he spoke.

Of Schnitzler nothing was heard, and the others could not tell if he were still alive.

But while this terrible scene was passing, Schnitzler had performed an act of the highest bravery. First he had tried, by using his axe, to climb out of the icy prison where he hung. This he could not do, so steadying himself against the glassy wall, he deliberately cut himself loose from the rope. He dropped to the floor of the crevasse, which, luckily, was not of extraordinary depth, and being uninjured, he set himself to find a way out. He followed the crevasse along its entire length, and discovered a little ledge of ice, with the aid of which, panting and exhausted, he reached the surface.

But even with Schnitzler's help it was impossible to raise Herr Nasse out of the chasm. The rope had cut deeply into the snow. He hung underneath an eave of the soft surface and could not be moved. Another willing helper, an Englishman, now came up, and after a time the body—for Herr Nasse had not survived—was lowered to the floor of the crevasse. Every effort was made to restore animation, but with no result, and there was nothing left to do but leave that icy grave and descend to the valley. Herr Nasse had suffered from a weak heart and an attack of pleurisy, and these gave him but a poor chance of withstanding the terrible pressure of the rope. Dr Scriven, from whose spirited translation from the German I have taken my facts, remarks that, "The death of Professor Nasse seems to emphasize a warning, already painfully impressed on us by the loss of Mr Norman Neruda, that there are special dangers awaiting those whose vital organs are not perfectly sound, and who undertake the exertion and fatigue of long and difficult climbs."

CHAPTER XIV

A WONDERFUL FEAT BY TWO LADIES

One of the highest and hardest passes in the Alps is the Sesia-Joch, 13,858 feet high, near Monte Rosa. The well-known mountaineer, Mr Ball, writing in 1863, referred to its first passage by Messrs George and Moore, as "amongst the most daring of Alpine exploits," and expressed a doubt whether it would ever be repeated. The party went *up* the steep Italian side (on the other, or Swiss side, it is quite easy). We can, therefore, judge of the astonishment of the members of the Alpine Club when they learnt that in 1869 "two ladies had not only crossed this most redoubtable of glacier passes, but crossed it from Zermatt to Alagna, thus descending the wall of rock, the ascent of which had until then been looked on as an extraordinary feat for first-rate climbers." The following extract from an Italian paper, aided by the notes communicated by the Misses Pigeon to *The Alpine Journal*, fully explains how this accidental but brilliant feat of mountaineering was happily brought to a successful termination.

"On 11th August 1869, Miss Anna and Miss Ellen Pigeon, of London, were at the Riffel Hotel, above Zermatt, with the intention of making the passage of the Lys-Joch on the next day, in order to reach Gressonay. Starting at 3 A.M. on the 12th, accompanied by Jean Martin, guide of Sierre, and by a porter, they arrived at 4 A.M. at the Gorner Glacier, which they crossed rapidly to the great plateau, enclosed between the Zumstein-Spitz, Signal-Kuppe, Parrot-Spitze, and Lyskamm, where they arrived at 10 A.M. At this point, instead of bearing to the right, which is the way to the Lys-Joch, they turned too much towards the left, so that they found themselves on a spot at the extremity of the plateau, from which they saw beneath their feet a vast and profound precipice, terminating at a great depth upon a glacier. The guide had only once, about four years before, crossed the Lys-Joch, and in these desert and extraordinary places, where no permanent vestiges remain of previous passages, he had not remembered the right direction, nor preserved a very clear idea of the localities. At the sight of the tremendous precipice he began to doubt whether he might not have mistaken the way, and, to form a better judgment, he left the ladies on the Col, half-stiffened with cold from the violence of the north wind, ascended to the Parrot-Spitze, and advanced towards the Ludwigshöhe, in order to examine whether along this precipice, which lay inexorably in front, there might be a place where a passage could be effected. But wherever he turned his eyes he saw nothing but broken rocks and couloirs yet more precipitous.

"In returning to the Col after his fruitless exploration, almost certain that he had lost his way, he saw among some *débris* of rock, an empty bottle (which had been placed there by Messrs George and Moore in 1862). This discovery persuaded him that here must be the pass, since some one in passing by the place had there deposited this bottle. He then applied himself to examining with greater attention the rocks below, and thought he saw a possibility of descending by them. He proposed this to the ladies, and they immediately commenced operations. All being tied together, at proper intervals, with a strong rope, they began the perilous descent, sometimes over the naked rock, sometimes over more or less extensive slopes of ice, covered with a light stratum of snow, in which steps had to be cut. It was often necessary to stop, in order to descend one after the other by means of the rope to a point where it might be possible to rest without being held up. The tremendous precipice was all this time under their eyes, seeming only to increase as they descended. This arduous and perilous exertion had continued for more than seven hours when, towards 6 P.M., the party arrived at a point beyond which all egress seemed closed. Slippery and almost perpendicular rocks beneath, right and left, and everywhere; near and around not a space sufficient to stretch one's self upon, the sun about to set, night at hand! What a position for the courageous travellers, and for the poor guide on whom devolved the responsibility of the fatal consequences which appeared inevitable!

"Nevertheless, Jean Martin did not lose his courage. Having caused the ladies to rest on the rocks, he ran right and left, climbing as well as he could, in search of a passage. For about half an hour he looked and felt for a way, but in vain. At length it appeared to him that it would be possible to risk a long descent by some rough projections which occurred here and there in the rocks. With indescribable labour, and at imminent peril of rolling as shapeless corpses into the crevasses of the glacier below, the travellers at length set foot upon the ice. It was 8 P.M.; they had commenced the descent at 11 A.M.; they crossed the Sesia Glacier at a running pace, on account of the increasing darkness of the night, which scarcely allowed them to distinguish the crevasses. After half an hour they set foot on *terra firma* at the moraine above the Alp of Vigne, where they perceived at no great distance a light, towards which they quickly directed their steps. The shepherd, named Dazza Dionigi, received them kindly, and lodged them for the night. Until they arrived at the Alp, both the ladies and the guide believed that they had made the pass of the Lys-Joch, and that they were now upon an Alp of Gressonay. It was, therefore, not without astonishment that they learned from the shepherd that, instead of this, they were at the head of the Val Sesia, and that they had accomplished the descent of the formidable Sesia-Joch."

EXTERIOR OF A CLIMBER'S HUT.

INTERIOR OF A CLIMBER'S HUT.

As an accompaniment to the foregoing highly-coloured narrative, the following modest notes, sent to *The Alpine Journal* by the Misses Pigeon, will be read with interest:

"All mountaineers are aware how much the difficulty of a pass is lessened or increased by the state of the weather. In this we were greatly favoured. For some days it had been very cold and wet at the Riffel; and when we crossed the Sesia-Joch we found sufficient snow in descending the ice-slope to give foothold, which decreased the labour of cutting steps—the axe was only brought into requisition whenever we traversed to right or left. Had the weather been very hot we should have been troubled with rolling stones. It was one of those clear, bright mornings so favourable for mountain excursions. Our guide had only once before crossed the Lys-Joch, four years previously, and on a very misty day. We were, therefore, careful to engage a porter who professed to know the way. The latter proved of no use whatever except to carry a knapsack.

"We take the blame to ourselves of missing the Lys-Joch; for, on making the discovery of the porter's ignorance, we turned to *Ball's Guide Book*, and repeatedly translated to Martin a passage we found there, warning travellers to avoid keeping too much to the right near the Lyskamm. The result of our interference was that Martin kept too much to the left, and missed the Lys-Joch altogether.

"When we perceived the abrupt termination of the actual Col, we all ascended, with the aid of step-cutting, along the slope of the Parrot-Spitze, until we came to a place where a descent seemed feasible. Martin searched for a better passage, but, after all, we took to the ice-slope, at first, for a little way, keeping on the rocks. Finding the slope so very rapid, we doubted whether we could be right in descending it; for we remembered that the descent of the Lys-Joch is described by Mr Ball as *easy*. We therefore retraced our steps up the slope to our former halting-place, thus losing considerable time, for it was now twelve o'clock. Then it was that Martin explored the Parrot-Spitze still further, and returned in three-quarters of an hour fully persuaded that there was no other way. We re-descended the ice-slope, and lower down crossed a couloir, and then more snow-slopes and rocks brought us to a lower series of rocks, where our passage seemed stopped at five o'clock. Here the mists, which had risen since the morning, much impeded our progress, and we halted, hoping they would disperse. Martin again went off on an exploring expedition, whilst the porter was sent in another direction. As both returned from a fruitless search, and sunset was approaching, the uncomfortable suggestion was made that the next search would be for the best sleeping quarters. However, Martin himself investigated the rocks pronounced impracticable by the porter, and by these we descended to the Sesia Glacier without unusual difficulty. When once fairly on the glacier, we crossed it at a running pace, for it was getting dark, and we feared to be benighted on the glacier. It was dark as we scrambled along the moraine on the other side, and over rocks and grassy knolls till the shepherd's light at Vigne gave us a happy indication that a shelter was not far off. The shouts of our guide brought the shepherd with his oil-lamp to meet us, and it was a quarter to nine o'clock P.M. when we entered his hut. After partaking of a frugal meal of bread and milk, we were glad to accept his offer of a hay bed, together with the unexpected luxury of sheets. When relating the story of our arrival to the Abbé Farinetti on the following Sunday at Alagna, the shepherd said that so great was his astonishment at the sudden apparition of travellers from that direction, that he thought it must be a visit of angels.

"We consider the Italian account incorrect as to the time we occupied in the descent. We could not have left our halting-place near the summit for the second time before a quarter to one o'clock, and in eight hours we were in this shepherd's hut.

"The Italian account exaggerates the difficulty we experienced. The rope was never used 'to hold up the travellers and let them down one by one.' On the contrary, one lady went *last*, preferring to see the awkward porter in front of her rather than behind. At one spot we came to an abrupt wall of rock and there we gladly availed ourselves of our guide's hand. The sensational sentence about 'rolling as shapeless corpses into the crevasses' is absurd, as we were at that juncture rejoicing in the prospect of a happy termination of our dilemma, and of crossing the glacier in full enjoyment of our senses."

The editor of *The Alpine Journal* concludes with the following comments:

"It is impossible to pass over without some further remark the behaviour of the guide and porter who shared this adventure. Jean Martin, if he led his party into a scrape, certainly showed no small skill and perseverance in carrying them safely out of it. Porters have as a class, and with some honourable exceptions, long afforded a proof that Swiss peasants are not necessarily born climbers. Their difficulties and blunders have, indeed, served as one of the standing jokes of Alpine literature. But we doubt if any porter has ever exhibited himself in so ignoble a position as the man who, having begun by obtaining an engagement under false pretences, ended by allowing one of his employers, a lady, to descend the Italian side of the Sesia-Joch last on the rope."

A PERILOUS CLIMB

In the year 1865 but few different routes were known up Mont Blanc. It has now been ascended from every direction and by every conceivable combination of routes, yet I doubt if any at all rivalling the one I intend quoting the account of has ever been accomplished. The route in question is by the Brenva Glacier on the Italian side of the great mountain, and the travellers who undertook to attempt what the guides hardly thought a possible piece of work, consisted of Mr Walker, his son Horace, Mr Mathews, and Mr Moore, the account which I take from *The Alpine Journal* having been written by the latter. For guides they had two very first-rate men, Melchior Anderegg and his cousin, Jacob Anderegg.

I shall omit the first part of the narrative, interesting though it is, and go at once to the point where, not long after sunrise, the mountaineers found themselves.

"We had risen very rapidly, and must have been at an elevation of more than 12,000 feet. Our position, therefore, commanded an extensive view in all directions. The guides were in a hurry, so cutting our halt shorter than would have been agreeable, we resumed our way at 7.55, and after a few steps up a slope at an angle of 50°, found ourselves on the crest of the buttress, and looking down upon, and across, the lower part of a glacier tributary to the Brenva, beyond which towered the grand wall of the Mont Maudit. We turned sharp to the left along the ridge, Jacob leading, followed by Mr Walker, Horace, Mathews, Melchior, and myself last. We had anticipated that, assuming the possibility of gaining the ridge on which we were, there would be no serious difficulty in traversing it, and so much as we could see ahead led us to hope that our anticipations would turn out correct. Before us lay a narrow but not steep arête of rock and snow combined, which appeared to terminate some distance in front in a sharp peak. We advanced cautiously, keeping rather below the top of the ridge, speculating with some curiosity on what lay beyond this peak. On reaching it, the apparent peak proved not to be a peak at all, but the extremity of the narrowest and most formidable ice arête I ever saw, which extended almost on a level for an uncomfortably long distance. Looking back by the light of our subsequent success, I have always considered it a providential circumstance that, at this moment, Jacob, and not Melchior was leading the party. In saying this, I shall not for an instant be suspected of any imputation upon Melchior's courage. But in him that virtue is combined to perfection with the equally necessary one of prudence, while he shares the objection which nearly all guides have to taking upon themselves, without discussion, responsibility in positions of doubt. Had he been in front, I believe that, on seeing the nature of the work before us, we should have halted and discussed the propriety of proceeding; and I believe further that, as the result of that discussion, our expedition would have then and there come to an end. Now in Jacob, with courage as faultless as Melchior's, and physical powers even superior, the virtue of prudence is conspicuous chiefly from its absence; and, on coming to this ugly place, it never for an instant occurred to him that we might object to go on, or consider the object in view not worth the risk which must be inevitably run. He therefore went calmly on without so much as turning to see what we thought of it, while I do not suppose that it entered into the head of any one of us spontaneously to suggest a retreat.

"On most arêtes, however narrow the actual crest may be, it is generally possible to get a certain amount of support by driving the pole into the slope on either side. But this was not the case here. We were on the top of a wall, the ice on the right falling vertically (I use the word advisedly), and on the left nearly so. On neither side was it possible to obtain the slightest hold with the alpenstock. I believe also that an arête of pure ice is more often encountered in description than in reality, that term being generally applied to hard snow. But here, for once, we had the genuine article, blue ice without a speck of snow on it. The space for walking was, at first, about the breadth of an ordinary wall, in which Jacob cut holes for the feet. Being last in the line I could see little of what was coming until I was close upon it, and was therefore considerably startled on seeing the men in front suddenly abandon the upright position, which in spite of the insecurity of the steps and difficulty of preserving the balance, had been hitherto maintained, and sit down *à cheval*. The ridge had narrowed to a knife edge, and for a few yards it was utterly impossible to advance in any other way. The foremost men soon stood up again, but when I was about to follow their example Melchior insisted emphatically upon my not doing so, but remaining seated. Regular steps could no longer be cut, but Jacob, as he went along, simply sliced off the top of the ridge, making thus a slippery pathway, along which those behind crept, moving one foot carefully after the other. As for me, I worked myself along with my hands in an attitude safer, perhaps, but considerably more uncomfortable, and, as I went, could not keep occasionally speculating, with an odd feeling of amusement, as to what would be the result if any of the party should chance to slip over on either side—what the rest would do— whether throw themselves over on the other side or not—and if so, what would happen then. Fortunately the occasion for the solution of this curious problem did not arise, and at 9.30 we reached the end of the arête, where it emerged in the long slopes of broken *névé*, over which our way was next to lie. As we looked back along our perilous path, it was hard to repress a shudder, and I think the dominant feeling of every man was one of wonder how the passage had been effected without accident. One good result, however, was to banish from Melchior's mind the last traces of doubt as to our ultimate success, his reply to our anxious enquiry whether he thought we should get up, being, 'We must, for we cannot go back.' In thus speaking, he probably said rather more than he meant, but the fact will serve to show that I have not exaggerated the difficulty we had overcome."

Mr Moore goes on to describe the considerable trouble the party had in mounting the extremely steep snow-slope on which they were now embarked. The continual step-cutting was heavy work for the guides. At last they were much annoyed to find between them and their goal "a great wall of ice running right across and completely barring the way upwards. Our position was, in fact, rather critical. Immediately over our heads the slope on which we were, terminated in a great mass of broken *séracs*, which might come down with a run at any moment. It seemed improbable that any way out of our difficulties would be found in that quarter. But, where else to look? There was no use in going to the left—to the right we *could* not go—and back we *would* not go. After careful scrutiny, Melchior thought it just possible that we might find a passage through those séracs on the higher and more level portion of the glacier to the right of them, and there being obviously no chance of success in any other direction, we turned towards them. The ice here was steeper and harder than it had yet been. In spite of all Melchior's care, the steps were painfully insecure, and we were glad to get a grip with one hand of the rocks alongside of which we passed. The risk, too, of an avalanche was considerable, and it was a relief when we were so close under the séracs that a fall from above could not well hurt us. Melchior had steered with his usual discrimination, and was now attacking the séracs at the only point where they appeared at all practical. Standing over the mouth of a crevasse choked with *débris*, he endeavoured to lift himself on to its upper edge, which was about 15 feet above. But to accomplish this seemed at first a task too great even for his agility, aided as it was by vigorous pushes. At last, by a marvellous exercise of skill and activity, he succeeded, pulled up Mr Walker and Horace, and then cast off the rope to reconnoitre, leaving them to assist Mathews, Jacob and myself in the performance of a similar manœuvre. We were all three still below, when a yell from Melchior sent a thrill through our veins. 'What is it?' said we to Mr Walker. A shouting communication took place between him and Melchior, and then came the answer, 'He says it is all right.' That moment was worth living for."

Mr Moore tells how, over now easy ground, the party rapidly ascended higher and higher. "We reached the summit at 3.10, and found ourselves safe at Chamouni at 10.30. Our day's work had thus extended to nearly 20 hours, of which 17½ hours were actual walking."

It is interesting to note that in after years a route was discovered on the opposite, or French side of Mont Blanc, of which the chief difficulty was an extremely narrow—but in this case also steep—ice ridge. This ascent, *via* the Aiguille de Bionnassay, enjoys, I believe, an even greater reputation than that by the Brenva. It has been accomplished twice by ladies, the first time by Miss Katherine Richardson, whose skill and extraordinary rapidity of pace have given her a record on more than one great peak. Miss Richardson, having done all the hard part of the climb, descended from the Dome de Gouter. The second ascent by a lady was undertaken successfully in 1899, by Mademoiselle Eugénie de Rochat, who has a brilliant list of climbs in the Mont Blanc district to her credit.

CHAPTER XV

A FINE PERFORMANCE WITHOUT GUIDES

The precipitous peak of the Meije, in Dauphiné, had long, like the Matterhorn, been believed inaccessible, and it was only after repeated attempts that at last the summit was reached. The direct route from La Bérarde will always be an extremely difficult climb to anyone who desires to do his fair share of the work; the descent of the great wall of rock is one of the few places I have been down, which took longer on the descent than on the ascent.

When the members of the Alpine Club heard that a party of Englishmen had succeeded, *without guides*, in making the expedition, they were much impressed by the feat, and on 17th December 1879, one of the climbers, Mr Charles Pilkington, read a paper before the Club describing his ascent. From it I quote the following. The party included the brothers Pilkington and Mr Gardiner.

The Meije is to the left, the Glacier Carré is the snow-patch on it, beneath this is the Great Wall.

ASCENDING A SNOWY WALL (page 216).

"On the 19th July 1878, we reached La Bérarde, where we found Mr Coolidge with the two Almers. Coolidge knew that we had come to try the Meije, and he had very kindly given us all the information he could, not only about it, but about several other peaks and passes in the district. Almer also, after finding out our plans, was good enough not to laugh at us, and gave us one or two useful hints. He told us as well that the difficulty did not so much consist in finding the way as in getting up it.

"At two o'clock in the afternoon of 20th July, we left for our bivouac in the Vallon des Etançons, taking another man with us besides our two porters, and at four reached the large square rock called the Hôtel Châteleret, after the ancient name of the valley. We determined to sleep here instead of at Coolidge's refuge a little higher up. The Meije was in full view, and we had our first good look at it since we had read the account of its ascent.

"We went hopefully to bed, telling our porters to call us at eleven the same evening, so as to start at midnight; but long before that it was raining hard, and it required all the engineering skill of the party and the india-rubber bag to keep the water out. It cleared up at daybreak. Of course it was far too late to start then; besides that, we had agreed not to make the attempt unless we had every sign of fine weather.

"As we had nothing else to do, we started at 8 A.M. on an exploring expedition, taking our spare ropes and some extra provisions, to leave, if possible, at M. Duhamel's cairn, some distance up the mountain, whilst our porters were to improve the refuge and lay in a stock of firewood. The snow was very soft, and we were rather lazy, so it was not until eleven that we reached the upper part of the Brêche Glacier, and were opposite our work. The way lies up the great southern buttress, which forms the eastern boundary of the Brêche Glacier, merging into the general face of the mountain about one-third of the total height from the Glacier des Etançons, and 700 feet below, and a little to the west of the Glacier Carré, from whence the final peak is climbed. The chief difficulty is the ascent from M. Duhamel's cairn, on the top of the buttress to the Glacier Carré.

"After a few steps up the snow, we gained the crest of the buttress by a short scramble. The crest is narrow, but very easy, and we went rapidly along, until we came to where a great break in the arête divides the buttress into an upper and a lower part; being no longer able to keep along the crest, we were forced to cross the rocks to our left to the couloir. Not quite liking the look of the snow, Gardiner asked us to hold tight whilst he tried it. Finding it all right he kicked steps up, and at five minutes past one we reached the cairn, having taken one hour and thirty-five minutes from the glacier. The great wall rose straight above us, but the way up, which we had had no difficulty in making out with the telescope from below, was no longer to be seen. Our spirits which had been rising during our ascent from the glacier, sunk once more, and our former uncertainty came back upon us; for it is difficult to imagine anything more hopeless-looking than this face of the Meije. It has been said that, after finding all the most promising ways impossible, this seeming impossibility was tried as a last chance. We looked at it a long time, but at last gave up trying to make out the way as a bad job, determined to climb where we could, if we had luck enough to get so far another day; so, leaving our spare ropes, a bottle of wine, a loaf of bread, and a tin of curried fowl carefully covered with stones, we made the best of our way back, reaching the glacier in one hour and twenty minutes, and our bivouac in an hour and a half more. There we spent the next night and following day, but at last we had to give in to the bad weather, and go sorrowfully down to La Bérarde. It was very disappointing. We had been looking forward to the attempt for more than six months. I had to leave in a few days for England. It was not a mountain for two men to be on alone; what if we had spent all our time and trouble for nothing, and only carried our bed and provisions to the cairn for someone else to use?

"On the evening of the 24th we were again at our bivouac; this time there was a cold north wind blowing, and the weather looked more settled than it had yet done since we came into the district. We watched the last glow of the setting sun fade on the crags of the Meije, and then crawled into our now well-known holes. At midnight exactly we were off, and, as we had much to carry, we took our porters with us as far as the bottom of the buttress, where we waited for daylight. At last the Tête du Replat opposite to us caught the reflection of the light, so, leaving a bottle of champagne for our return, as a reward of victory or consolation for defeat, we started at 3.15, unfortunately with an omen, for in bidding good-bye to our porters, we said 'adieu,' instead of 'au revoir, and though we altered the word at once, they left us with grave faces, old Lagier mournfully shaking his head. Gardiner took the lead again, and at 4.45 we once more stood beside the stone-man, finding our *cache* of provisions all safe. Here we rearranged our luggage. Both the others took heavy loads; Gardiner the knapsack, Lawrence the 200 feet of spare rope and our wine tin, holding three quarts; the sleeping bag only was given to me, as I was told off to lead.

"We got under weigh at 5.15, and soon clambered up the remaining part of the buttress, and reached the bottom of the great wall, the Glacier Carré being about 700 feet above us, and some distance to our right. We knew that from here a level traverse had to be made until nearly under the glacier before it was possible to turn upwards. We had seen a ledge running in the right direction; crossing some steep rocks and climbing over a projecting knob (which served us a nasty trick on our descent), we let ourselves gently down on to the ledge, leaving a small piece of red rag to guide us in coming back. The ledge, although 4 or 5 feet broad, was not all that could be wished, for it was more than half-covered with snow, which, as the ledge sloped outwards, was not to be trusted; the melting and refreezing of this had formed ice below, nearly covering the available space, forcing us to walk on the edge. We cut a step here and there. It improved as we went on, and when half-way across the face we were able to turn slightly upwards, and at 6.30 were near the spot where later in the day the icicles from the extreme western end of the Glacier Carré fall. It is not necessary to go right into the line of fire, and in coming back we kept even farther away than on the ascent.

"So far the way had been fairly easy to find, but now came the great question of the climb; how to get up the 600 feet of rock wall above us. To our right it rose in one sheer face, the icicles from the Glacier Carré, fringing the top; to our left the rocks, though not so steep, were very smooth, and at the top, especially to the right, near the glacier, they became precipitous. A little above us a bridge ledge led away to the left, slanting upwards towards the lowest and most practicable part of the wall, obviously the way up. Climbing to this ledge, we followed it nearly half-way back across the face, then the holding-places got fewer and more filled with ice, the outward slope more and more until at last its insecure and slippery look warned us off it, and we turned up the steeper but rougher rocks on our right. In doing so I believe we forsook the route followed by all our predecessors, but we were obliged to do so by the glazed state of the rocks.

"As the direction in which we were now going was taking us towards the glacier and the steep upper rocks, we soon turned again to our left to avoid them, the only way being up some smooth slabs, with very little hold, the sort of rocks where one's waistcoat gives a great deal of holding power; worming oneself up these we reached a small shelf where we were again in doubt. It was impossible to go straight up; to the left the rocks, though easier, only led to the higher part of the ledge we had forsaken; we spent some minutes examining this way, but again did not like the look of the glazed rocks; so we took the only alternative and went to the right. Keeping slightly upwards, we gained about 50 feet in actual height by difficult climbing. We were now getting on to the steep upper rocks near the glacier, which we had wanted to avoid.

"This last piece of the wall will always remain in our minds as the most desperate piece of work we have ever done; the rocks so far had been firm, but now, although far too steep for loose stones to lodge on, were so shattered that we dared not trust them; at the same time we had to be very careful, lest in removing any we should bring others down upon us.

"One place I shall never forget. Gardiner was below, on a small ledge, with no hand-hold to speak of, trying to look as if he could stand any pull; my brother on a knob a little higher up, to help me if necessary. I was able to pull myself about 8 feet higher, but the next rock was insecure, and the whole nearly perpendicular. A good many loose stones had been already pulled out; this one would not come. It is hard work tugging at a loose stone with one hand, the other in a crack, and only one foot finding anything to rest on. I looked down, told them how it was, and came down to rest.

"For about a minute nothing was said; all our faces turned towards the Glacier Carré, now only about 60 feet above us. We all felt it would have been hard indeed to turn back, yet it was not a pleasant place, and we could not see what was again above. We were on what may be fairly called a precipice. In removing the loose stones, the slightest backhanded jerk, just enough to miss the heads of the men behind, sent them clear into the air; they never touched anything for a long time after leaving the hand, and disappeared with a disagreeable hum on to the Glacier des Etançons, 1800 feet below. We looked and tried on both sides, but it was useless, so we went at it again. After the fourth or fifth attempt I managed to get up about 10 feet, to where there was some sort of hold; then my brother followed, giving me rope enough to get to a firm rock, where I remained till joined by the others. It was almost as bad above, but we crawled carefully up; one place actually overhung—fortunately there was plenty of hold, and we slung ourselves up it! From this point the rocks became rather easier, and at 9.30 we reached a small sloping shelf of rock, about 20 yards to the west of the Glacier Carré and on the top of the great rock wall. Stopping here for a short time to get cool, and to let one of the party down to get the axes, which had been tied to a rope and had caught in a crevice in the rock, we changed leaders, and crossing some shelving rocks, climbed up a gully, or cleft, filled with icicles, and reached the platform of rock at the south-west end of the Glacier Carré at 10.15 A.M.

"The platform we had reached can only be called one by comparison; it is rather smooth, and slopes too much to form a safe sleeping-place, but we left our extra luggage there.

"At 11.10 we started up the glacier, Gardiner going ahead, kicking steps into the soft, steep snow.

"We were much more cheerful now than we had been two hours before. My companions had got rid of their heavy loads, the day was still very fine, and Almer had told us that, could we but reach the glacier, we should have a good chance of success.

"Shortly before 1 P.M. we were underneath the well-known overhanging top, the rocks of which, cutting across the face, form a triangular corner. It is the spot where Gaspard lost so much time looking for the way on the first ascent. We knew that the arête had here to be crossed, and the northern face on the other side taken to.

"Almost before I got my head over the crest came the anxious question from below, 'Will it go on the other side?' I could not see, however; so when the others came up, Gardiner fixed himself and let us down to the full extent of the rope. The whole northern face, as far as we could see, looked terribly icy; but as there was no other way of regaining the arête higher up without going on to it, we told him to come down after us.

"Turning to the right as soon as possible, we had to traverse the steep, smooth face for a short distance. It took a long time, for the rocks were even worse than they had appeared; we often had to clear them of ice for a yard before we could find any hold at all and sometimes only the left hand could be spared for cutting. After about 50 yards of this work we were able to turn upwards, and with great difficulty wriggled up the slippery rocks leading to the arête; rather disgusted to find the north face so difficult—owing, perhaps, to the lateness of the season.

"It was our last difficulty, for the arête, though narrow, gives good hand and foot-hold, and we pressed eagerly onwards. In a few minutes it became more level, and there, sure enough, were the three stone-men, only separated from us by some easy rocks and snow, which we went at with a rush, and at 2.25 we stood on the highest point of the Meije.

"Knowing that it would be useless for us to try and descend further than the Glacier Carré that day, and as it was pleasanter on the top than there, we went in for a long halt. Untying the rope—for the top is broad enough to be safe— we examined the central cairn, where the tokens are kept. We found a tin box, containing the names of our predecessors; a bottle, hanging by a string, the property of Mr Coolidge; a tri-coloured flag; and a scented pocket-handkerchief belonging to M. Guillemin, still retaining its former fragrance, which it had not 'wasted on the desert air.' We tore a corner off each, leaving a red-and-yellow rag in exchange; put our names in the tin, and an English penny with a hole bored through it.

"Then, after repairing the rather dilapidated southern cairn, we sat down to smoke and enjoy the view, which the fact of the mountain standing on the outside of the group, the tremendous depth to which the eye plunges on each side, the expansive panorama of the Dauphiné and neighbouring Alps, and the beautiful distant view of the Pennine chain from Mont Blanc to Monte Rosa, combine to make one of the finest in the Alps.

"At four o'clock, after an hour and a half on the top, we started downwards, soon arriving at the spot where it was necessary to leave the arête; however, before doing so, we went along it to where it was cut off, to see if we could let ourselves straight down into the gap, and so avoid the detour by the northern face, but it was impracticable; so, putting the middle of the spare rope round a projecting rock on the arête, we let ourselves down to where we had gone along on the level, pulling the rope down after us; then regaining the gap by the morning's route, we crossed it, and leisurely descended the south-western face to the Glacier Carré, filling our now empty wine tin with water on the way down. We reached the glacier at 6.30. In skirting the base of the Pic du Glacier we found a nice hollow in the snow, which looked a good place to sleep in. Gardiner wanted one of us to stop and build a stone-wall, whilst the others fetched the bag and provisions from the bottom of the glacier. Lawrence was neutral; I was rather against it, having slept on snow before. At last we all went down to the rocky platform where our luggage had been left. We cleared a place for the bag, but it all sloped so much, and the edge of the precipice was so near, that we dared not lie down. We looked for a good rock to tie ourselves to; even that could not be found. Then some one thought we might scrape a hole in the steep snow above us, and get into it. That, of course, was quite out of the question. Nothing therefore remained for us but Gardiner's hollow above—the only level place we had seen above M. Duhamel's cairn large enough for us to lay our bag on. There was no time to be lost; it was getting dark; a sharp frost had already set in: so we at once shouldered our traps and trudged wearily up the glacier once more, wishing now that we had left somebody to build a wall.

"On reaching the hollow we put the ropes, axes, hats, and knapsack on the snow as a sort of carpet, placed the bag on the top, then, pulling off our boots for pillows, and putting on the comfortable woollen helmets given to us by Mrs Hartley, got into the bag to have our supper. Fortunately there was not much wind; but it was rather difficult to open the meat tin. We did as well as we could, however, and after supper tried to smoke; but the cold air got into the bag and made that a failure; so we looked at the scene instead.

"The moon was half full, and shone upon us as we lay, making everything look very beautiful. We could see the snow just in front of us, and then, far away through the frosty air all the mountains on the other side of the Vallon des Etançons, with the silver-grey peak of the Ecrins behind, its icy ridges standing out sharply against the clear sky; and deep down in the dark valley below was the signal fire of our porters. As this could only be seen by sitting bolt upright, we got tired of looking at it, and the last link connecting us with the lower world being broken, we felt our utter loneliness.

"The moon soon going behind a rocky spur of the Pic du Glacier, we lay down and tried to get warm by pulling the string round the neck of the bag as tight as possible and breathing inside; but somehow the outside air got in also. So closing it as well as we could, with only our heads out, we went to sleep, but not for long. The side on which we lay soon got chilled. Now, as the bag was narrow, we all had to face one way on account of our knees; so the one who happened to be the soonest chilled through would give the word, and we all turned together. I suppose we must have changed sides every half-hour through the long night. We got some sleep, however, and felt all right when the first glimmering of dawn came over the mountains on our left. As soon as we could see we had breakfast; but the curried fowl was frozen, and the bread could only be cut with difficulty, as a shivering seized one every minute. We had the greatest trouble in getting our boots on. They were pressed out of shape, and, in spite of having been under our heads, were hard frozen. At last, by burning paper inside, and using them as lantern for our candle, we thawed them enough to get them on, and then spent a quarter of an hour stamping about to thaw ourselves. We rolled the bag up and tied it fast to a projecting rock, hanging the meat tin near as a guide to anyone looking for it.

"At 4.30 we set off, very thankful that we had a fine day before us. We soon went down the glacier, and down and across to the shelf of rock where the real descent of the wall was to begin. A few feet below was a jagged tooth of rock which we could not move; so to it we tied one end of the 100 feet of rope, taking care to protect the rope where it pressed on the sharp edges, with pieces of an old handkerchief; the other end we threw over the edge, and by leaning over we could just see the tail of it on some rocks below the bad part, [9] so we knew it was long enough.

"After a short discussion we arranged to go down one at a time, as there were places where we expected to throw all our weight on the rope. Gardiner was to go first as he was the heaviest; my brother next, carrying all the traps and the three axes, as he had the strongest pair of hands and arms in the party; whilst I as the lightest, was to bring down the rear. So tying the climbing rope round his waist as an extra help, Gardiner started, whilst we paid it out. He soon disappeared, but we knew how he was getting on, and when he was in the worst places, by the 'Lower,' 'A little lower,' 'Hold,' 'Hold hard,' which came up from below, getting fainter as he got lower. Fifty feet of the rope passed through our hands before he stopped going. 'Can you hold there?' we asked. 'No. Hold me while I rest a little, and then give me 10 feet more if you can.' So after a while we got notice to lower, and down he went again until nearly all our rope was gone; then it slackened. He told us he was fast, and that we could pull up the rope.

"Then Lawrence shouldered his burdens, the three axes being tied below him with a short piece of rope. The same thing happened again, only it was more exciting, for every now and then the axes caught and loosened with a jerk, which I felt on the rope I was paying out, although it was tied to him. At first I thought it was a slip, but soon got used to it. Lawrence did not go so far as Gardiner, but stopped to help me at the bottom of the worst piece.

"It was now my turn. Tying the other end of the loose rope round me, I crawled cautiously down to where the tight rope was fixed. The others told me afterwards they did not like it. I certainly did not. The upper part was all right; but lower down the rocks were so steep that if I put much weight on the rope it pulled me off them, and gave a tendency to swing over towards the Glacier Carré, which, as only one hand was left for climbing with, was rather difficult to resist. I remember very well sitting on a projecting rock, with nothing below it but air for at least 100 feet. Leaving this, Lawrence half pulled me towards him with the loose rope. A few steps more and I was beside him, and we descended together to Gardiner, cutting off the fixed rope high up, so as to leave as little as possible, and in a few minutes more we all three reached the small shelf of rocks above the smooth slabs by which we had descended the day before. It was the place where we had spent some time trying to avoid the steep bit we had just descended, and which had taken us nearly two hours.

"This ledge is about 3 feet broad. We had got down the only place on the mountain that had given us any anxiety. It was warm and pleasant; all the day was before us; so we took more than an hour to lunch and rest.

"On starting again we ought to have stuck to our old route and descended by the slabs, as we could easily have done; but after a brief discussion we arranged to take a short cut, by fixing a second rope and letting ourselves straight down the drop on to the lower slanting ledge, at a point a few feet higher than where we had left it on the ascent.

"We descended one at a time, as before, and, what with tying and untying, took much longer than we should have done had we gone the other way. On gaining the ledge we turned to our left and soon came across one of our marks; then striking down sooner than our old route would have taken us, we gave a wider berth to the falling ice, and got into the traverse leading to the top of the buttress. Along it we went; but it looked different, had less snow, and when we came near the end a steep rock, with a nasty drop below, blocked the way. It appeared so bad that I said we were wrong. As the others were not sure, we retraced our steps, and by a very difficult descent gained a lower ledge. There was no snow on this, but the melting of the snow above made the rocks we had to take hold of so wet that we often got a stream of water down our arms and necks.

"At last, after nearly crossing, it became quite impossible, and we turned back, having gained nothing but a wetting.

"Below it was far too steep. Immediately above was the place we had tried just before. We could not make it out; we had been so positive about the place above.

"We were just thinking of trying it again more carefully, when Lawrence pointed up at something, and there, sure enough, was the bit of red rag left the day before to show the commencement of the traverse.

"We marked where it was, and then crawled back along the ledge on which we were. Scrambling up the steep drop, we made quickly upwards, and, turning towards our flag, found that the only way to it was along the very ledge where we had first tried, and which proved to be the traverse after all.

"We were very glad to get into it once more, as for the last three hours we had been on the look-out for falling ice. Some had already shot over our heads, sending showers of splinters on to us, and one piece as big as one's fist had come rather closer than was pleasant. On our left, the Glacier Carré kept up a regular fire of it, the ice following with tremendous noise on to the rocks below. Every time it gave us a start, as we could not always see at once where the fall had taken place; and although the danger was more imaginary than real, it is not pleasant to be constantly on the look-out, and flattening one's self against the rocks to avoid being hit.

"We soon crossed the snowy part of the traverse, and were again in front of the rock which had turned us back before. It looked no better; but on going close up we found a small crack near the top, just large enough to get our fingers into, giving excellent hold. By this we swung ourselves up and across the worst part.

"We thought we had only two hours more easy descent, and our work would be done. But we made a mistake.

"At first we went rapidly down, and were soon cheered by the sight of M. Duhamel's cairn, looking about five minutes off. I was in front at the time, and was just getting on to a short snow-slope by which we had ascended the day before, when, doubting its safety, I asked the others to hold fast whilst I tried it. The moment I put my foot on the snow, all the top went away, slowly at first, then, taking to the left, went down the couloir with a rush. We tried again where the upper layer had gone away, but it was all unsafe; so we had to spend half an hour getting down the rocks, where we had ascended in ten minutes, and it was not until 2.30 that we reached the cairn.

"It was 3.30 before we continued the descent. The couloir was not in good order and required care. Gardiner, who was in front, did not get on as well as usual. At last, thinking we might get impatient, he showed us his fingers, which were bleeding in several places, and awfully raw and sore. He had pluckily kept it all to himself until the real difficulties were over; but the snow of the couloir had softened his hands, and these last rocks were weathered granite, and very sharp and cutting; so he had to go very gingerly.

"At the bottom of the buttress a surprise awaited us, for as we descended the last 20 feet, the weather-beaten face of old Lagier, our porter, appeared above the rocks. The faithful old fellow said he had traced our descent by the occasional flashing of the wine tin in the sun, and had come alone to meet us, bringing us provisions as he thought we might have run short. He had waited six hours for us, and had iced the bottle of champagne which had been left on the ascent. We opened it and then hurried down to the glacier, taking off the rope at the moraine, and ran all the rest of the way on the snow to our bivouac, like a lot of colts turned loose in a field, feeling it a great relief to get on to something on which we could tumble about as we liked without falling over a precipice."

That the Meije is a really difficult mountain may be assumed from the fact that for some years after its first ascent, no party succeeded in getting up and down it on the same day. When every step of the way became well known, of course much quicker times were possible, and when, on 16th September

1892, I went up it with the famous Dauphiné guide, Maximin Gaspard, and Roman Imboden (the latter aged twenty-three, and perhaps the finest rock climber in Switzerland), we had all in our favour. There was neither ice nor snow on the rocks, and no icicles hung from the Glacier Carré, while the weather was still and cloudless. We slept at the bottom of the buttress—just at the spot where Mr Pilkington met his porter—and from here were exactly four hours (including a halt of one hour) reaching the top of the Meije.

It is now the fashion to cross the Meije from La Bérarde to La Grave, the descent on the other side being also extremely hard. For a couple of hours after leaving the summit a narrow ridge is traversed with several formidable gaps in it.

CHAPTER XVI

THE PIZ SCERSCEN TWICE IN FOUR DAYS—THE FIRST ASCENT OF MONT BLANC BY A WOMAN.

It was a mad thing to do. I realised that when thinking of it afterwards; but this is how it happened.

I had arranged with a friend, Mr Edmund Garwood, to try a hitherto unattempted route on a mountain not far from Maloja. He was to bring his guide, young Roman Imboden; I was to furnish a second man, Wieland, of St Moritz.

WIELAND ON THE HIGHEST POINT OF PIZ SCERSCEN (page 200).

A Party on a Mountain Top.

The other Party Descending Piz Bernina (page 202).

A Party commencing the Descent of a Snow Ridge.

The hour had come to start, the carriage was at the door and the provisions were in it, and Wieland and I were in readiness when, to our surprise, Roman turned up without Mr Garwood. A note which he brought explained that the latter was not well, but hoped I would make the expedition all the same, and take Roman with me. I was unwilling to monopolise a new ascent, though probably only an easy one, so I refused to go till my friend was better, and asked the guides to suggest something else. The weather was lovely and our food ready, and it seemed a pity to waste either.

Wieland could not think of a suitable climb, so I turned to Roman, who had only arrived at Pontresina two days before, and asked him his ideas.

He very sensibly inquired: "What peaks have you not done yet here, ma'am?"

"All but the Scerscen."

"Then we go for the—whatever you call it."

"Oh, but Roman," I exclaimed, "the Scerscen is very difficult, and there is 3 feet of fresh snow on the mountains, and it is out of the question!"

"I don't believe any of these mountains are difficult," said Roman doggedly, with that contempt for all Engadine climbing shown by guides from the other side of Switzerland.

"Ask Wieland," I suggested.

Wieland smiled at the question, and said he did not at all mind going to look at the Scerscen, but, as to ascending it under the present conditions, of course it was absurd.

"Besides," he added, "we are much too late to go to the Marinelli Hut to-day."

"Why not do it from the Mortel Hut?" I remarked, on the "in for a penny in for a pound" principle.

He smiled again; indeed, I think he laughed, and agreed that, as anyhow we could not go up the Scerscen, we might as well sleep at the Mortel Hut as anywhere else.

"Have you ever been up it?" Roman inquired.

Wieland answered that he had not. Roman turned to me: "Can you find the mountain? Should you know it if you saw it? Don't let us go up the wrong one, ma'am!"

I promised to lead them to the foot of the peak, and Roman repeated his conviction that all Engadine mountains were perfectly easy, and that we should find ourselves on the top of the Scerscen next morning. However, he made no objection to taking an extra rope of 100 feet, and, telling one friend our plan in strictest confidence, we climbed into the carriage.

We duly arrived at the Mortel Hut and were early in bed, as Roman wished us to set out at an early hour, or a late one, if I may thus allude to 11 P.M. He was still firmly convinced that to the top of the Scerscen we should go, and wanted every moment in hand, in spite of his recent criticisms of Engadine mountains. There was a very useful moon, and by its light we promised Roman to take him to the foot of the peak, where its rocky sides rise abruptly from the Scerscen Glacier.

I must here explain that there are several ways up the Scerscen. I wished to ascend by the rocks on the south side, which, though harder, were safer than the other routes. As for the descent (if we got up!) we intended coming down the way we had ascended, little knowing not only that no one had been down by this route, but also that a party had attempted to get down it and had been driven back. As for finding our way up, some notes in the *Alpine Journal* were our only guide. The mountain had been previously ascended but a few times altogether, and only, I think, once or twice by the south face. No lady had up till then tried it.

We were off punctually at 11 P.M., and by the brilliant light of the moon made good time over the glacier and up the snow slopes leading to the Sella Pass. This we reached in three hours, without a pause, from the hut, and, making no halt there, immediately plunged into the softer snow on the Italian side, and began to skirt the precipices on our left. Even in midsummer, it was still dark at this early hour, and the moon had already set. A great rocky peak rose near us, and Wieland gave it as his opinion that it was the Scerscen. I differed from him, believing our mountain to be some distance farther, so it was mutually agreed that we should halt for food, after which we should have more light to enable us to determine our position.

Gradually the warmth of dawn crept over the sky, and soon the beautiful spectacle of an Alpine sunrise was before us, with the wonderful "flush of adoration" on the mountain heads. There was no doubt now where we were; our peak was some way beyond, and the only question was, how to go up it? I repeated to Roman the information I had gleaned from the Journal, and he thanked me, doubtless having his own ideas, which he intended alone to be guided by. Luckily, as we advanced the mountain became visible from base to summit, so that Roman could trace out his way up it as upon a map. We walked up the glacier to the foot of the mighty wall, and soon began to go up it, advancing for some time with fair rapidity, in spite of the fresh snow. After, perhaps, a couple of hours or so, we came to our first real difficulty. This was a tall, red cliff, with a cleft up part of it, and, as there was an evil-looking and nearly perpendicular gully of ice to the right and overhanging rocks to the left, we had either to go straight up or abandon the expedition. The cleft was large and was garnished with a sturdy icicle, or column of ice, some 5 feet or more in diameter. Bidding me wedge myself into a firm place, Roman began to cut footholds up the icicle, and then, when after a few steps the cleft or chimney ended, he turned to his right and wormed himself along the very face of the cliff, holding on by the merest irregularities, which can hardly be termed ledges. After a couple of yards he struck straight up, and wriggling somehow on the surface, rendered horribly slippery by the snow, he at last, after what seemed an age, called on Wieland to follow. What was a *tour de force* for the first man was comparatively easy for the second, and soon my turn came to try my hand—or rather my feet and knees and any other adhesive portion of my person—on the business. The first part was the worst, for, as the rope came from the side and not above till the traverse was made, I had no help. Eventually I, too, emerged on to the wall, and saw right over me the rope passing through a gap, behind which, excellently placed, were the guides. I helped myself to the utmost of my capacity, but a pull was not unwelcome towards the end, when, exhausted and breathless, I could struggle no more. As I joined the guides they moved to give me space on the ledge, and we spent a well-earned quarter of an hour in rest and refreshment. The worst was now over, but owing to the snow, which covered much of the rock to a depth of about 2 or 3 feet, the remainder of the way was distinctly difficult, and as the mountain was totally unknown to us we never could tell what troubles might be in store. However, having left the foot of the actual peak at 5.40 A.M., we arrived on the top at 10.40 A.M., and as we lifted our heads above the final rocks, hardly daring to believe that we really were on the summit, a distant cheer was borne to our ears from Piz Bernina, and we knew that our arrival had been observed by another party.

So formidable did we consider the descent that we only allowed ourselves ten minutes on the top, and then we prepared to go. Could we cross the ridge to Piz Bernina and so avoid the chimney? It had a great reputation, and we feared to embark on the unknown. So at 10.50 A.M. we began the descent, moving one at a time with the utmost caution. Before long the difficulties increased as we reached the steeper part of the mountain. The rocks now streamed with water from the rapidly melting snow, under the rays of an August sun. As I held on, streams ran in at my wristbands, and soon I was soaked through. But the work demanded such close attention that a mere matter of discomfort was nothing. Presently we had to uncoil our spare 100 feet of rope, and now our progress grew slower and slower. After some hours we came to the chimney. No suitable rock could be found to attach the rope to, so Roman sat down and thought the matter out. The difficulty was to get the last man down; for the two first, held from above, the descent was easy. Roman soon hit upon an ingenious idea. Wieland and I were to go down to the bottom of the cleft. Wieland was to unrope me and, leaving me, was to cut steps *across* the ice-slope to our left till leverage was obtainable for the rope across the boss of rock where Roman stood, and where it would remain in position so long as it was kept taut, with Roman at one end and Wieland slowly paying out from below. The manœuvre succeeded, and after about two hours' work Wieland had hewn a large platform in the ice and prepared to gradually let out the rope as Roman came down. He descended in grand form, puffing at his pipe and declared the difficulty grossly over-rated, though he did not despise the precaution. At 2.30 A.M. we re-entered the Mortel Hut, somewhat tired, but much pleased with the success of our expedition.

Our second ascent of Piz Scerscen is soon told.

Four days later Roman casually remarked to me: "It is a pity, ma'am, we have not crossed the Scerscen to the Bernina."

"It is," I replied. "Let us start at once and do it."

Wieland was consulted, and was only too delighted to go anywhere under Roman's leadership. Our times will give an idea of the changed state of the mountain, for, leaving the Mortel Hut at 12.30 midnight, we were on the top of the Scerscen at 8 A.M. At nine we set off, and taking things leisurely, with halts for food, we passed along the famous arête, and, thanks to Roman's choice of route, met with not one really hard step. At 2.30 P.M. we found ourselves on the top of Piz Bernina, and had a chat with another party, who had arrived not long before. I waited to see them start, and rejoiced that I had kept two plates. Then we, too, set forth, and were in the valley by 7 P.M.

THE FIRST ASCENT OF MONT BLANC BY A WOMAN, AND SOME SUBSEQUENT ASCENTS

The first woman who reached the summit of Mont Blanc was a native of Chamonix, Maria Paradis by name. Her account of her expedition is so admirably graphic and picturesque that I shall give a translation of it as like the original as I can. Though it was so far back as the year 1809, Maria writes quite in the spirit of modern journalism.

She begins:—"I was only a poor servant. One day the guides said to me, 'We are going up there, come with us. Travellers will come and see you afterwards and give you presents.' That decided me, and I set out with them. When I reached the Grand Plateau I could not walk any longer. I felt very ill, and I lay down on the snow. I panted like a chicken in the heat. They held me up by my arms on each side and dragged me along. But at the Rochers-Rouge I could get no further, and I said to them 'Chuck me into a crevasse and go on yourselves.'

"'You must go to the top,' answered the guides. They seized hold of me, they dragged me, they pushed me, they carried me, and at last we arrived. Once at the summit, I could see nothing clearly, I could not breathe, I could not speak."

Maria was thirty years of age, and made quite a fortune out of her achievement. From that time, tourists returning from Mont Blanc noticed with surprise, as they passed through the pine woods, a feast spread out under the shade of a huge tree. Cream, fruit, etc., were tastefully displayed on the white cloth. A neat-looking peasant woman urged them to partake. "It is Maria of Mont Blanc!" the guides would cry, and the travellers halted to hear the story of her ascent and to refresh themselves.

The second woman, and the first lady to climb Mont Blanc, was a Frenchwoman, Mademoiselle d'Angeville. For years she had determined to make the attempt, but it was only in 1838, when she was 44 years of age, that she came to Chamonix with the intention of immediately setting out for the great mountain. She had many difficulties to surmount. The guides feared the responsibility of taking up a woman, many of the Chamonix people thought her mad, and while one was ready to offer a thousand francs to five that she would not reach the top, another was prepared to accept heavy odds that there would be a catastrophe. At last, however, all was ready, and she started. Two other parties offered to join her. She declined with thanks. After half an hour on the glacier she detached herself from the rope and would accept no help. This was far from being out of sheer bravado, it was simply that she desired to inspire confidence in her powers. During the night on the rocks of the Grands Mulets she suffered terribly from cold and could not snatch a moment's sleep. When the party stopped for breakfast at the Grand Plateau, she could eat nothing. At the Corridor, feverishness, and fearful thirst overcame her; she fell to the ground from weakness and drowsiness. After a little rest, however, she was able to go on, but at the Mur de la Cote she felt desperately ill. Violent palpitation seized on her and her limbs felt like lead. With a tremendous effort she moved on. The beatings of her heart became more suffocating, her pulse was too rapid to count, she could not take more than ten steps without stopping. One thing only remained strong in her—the *will*. During these frequent halts she heard the murmuring of talk between the guides, as in a dream. "We shall fail! Look at her, she has fallen asleep! Shall we try and carry her?" while Couttet cried, "If ever I find myself again with a lady on Mont Blanc!" At these words Mademoiselle d'Angeville, with a desperate effort, shook off her torpor and stood up. She clung with desperate energy to the one idea: "If I die," she said to the guides, "promise to carry me up there and bury me on the top!" And the men, stupified with such persistence, answered gravely, "Make your mind easy, mademoiselle, you shall go there, dead or alive!"

HARD WORK.

MRS AUBREY LE BLOND SETS OUT IN A LONG SKIRT
(page 87).

As she approached the top she felt better, and was able to advance without support, and when she stepped on to the summit, and knew that her great wish was at last accomplished, all sensation of illness vanished as if by enchantment.

"And now, mademoiselle, you shall go higher than Mont Blanc!" exclaimed the guides, and joining hands they lifted her above their shoulders.

One more ascent by a lady deserves mention here, that of Miss Stratton, on 31st January 1876. She was the first person to reach the summit of Mont Blanc in mid-winter.

It is difficult to understand why these early climbers of Mont Blanc, men as well as women, suffered so terribly from mountain sickness, a disease one rarely hears of nowadays in the Alps. The question is too vexed a one for me to discuss it here, but I may say that want of training and unsuitable food bring it on in most cases. "The stagnation of the air in valleys above the snow-line," was believed to produce it, and I cannot help thinking that this does have some effect. The first time I went up Mont Blanc I did not feel well on the Grand Plateau, but was all right when I reached the breezy ridge of the Bosses. The second time, ascending by the route on the Italian side of the peak, where there are no snowy valleys, I did not suffer at all. The third time I felt uncomfortable on the slope leading to the Corridor, but quite myself again above.

CHAPTER XVII

THE ASCENT OF A WALL OF ICE

Of all the writers on Alpine matters none has a more charming style, or has described his adventures in a more modest manner, than Sir Leslie Stephen. Perhaps the most delightful passages in his *Playground of Europe* are those in which he tells how, in company with the Messrs Mathews, he managed to get up the great wall of ice between the Mönch and the Eiger, known as the Eigerjoch. The Messrs Mathews had with them two Chamonix guides, while Mr Leslie Stephen had engaged the gigantic Oberlander Ulrich Lauener. In those days there was often keen rivalry—and something more—between French and German-speaking guides, and Lauener was apt to be rather an autocrat on the mountains. "As, however, he could not speak a word of French, nor they of German, he was obliged to convey his 'sentiments' in pantomime, which, perhaps, did not soften 'their vigour.' I was accordingly prepared for a few disputes next day.

"About four on the morning of 7th August we got off from the inn on the Wengern Alp, notwithstanding a few delays, and steered straight for the foot of the Eiger. In the early morning the rocks around the glacier and the lateral moraines were hard and slippery. Before long, however, we found ourselves well on the ice, near the central axis of the Eiger Glacier, and looking up at the great terrace-shaped ice-masses, separated by deep crevasses, which rose threateningly over our heads, one above another, like the defences of some vast fortification. And here began the first little dispute between Oberland and Chamouni. The Chamouni men proposed a direct assault on the network of crevasses above us. Lauener said that we ought to turn them by crossing to the south-west side, immediately below the Mönch. My friends and their guides forming a majority, and seeming to have little respect for the arguments urged by the minority, we gave in and followed them, with many muttered remarks from Lauener. We soon found ourselves performing a series of manœuvres like those required for the ascent of the Col du Géant. At times we were lying flat in little gutters on the faces of the *séracs*, worming ourselves along like boa-constrictors. At the next moment we were balancing ourselves on a knife-edge of ice between two crevasses, or plunging into the very bowels of the glacier, with a natural arch of ice meeting above our heads. I need not attempt to describe difficulties and dangers familiar to all ice-travellers. Like other such difficulties, they were exciting, and even rather amusing for a time, but, unfortunately, they seemed inclined to last rather too long. Some of the deep crevasses apparently stretched almost from side to side of the glacier, rending its whole mass into distorted fragments. In attempting to find a way through them, we seemed to be going nearly as far backwards as forwards, and the labyrinth in which we were involved was as hopelessly intricate after a long struggle as it had been at first. Moreover, the sun had long touched the higher snow-fields, and was creeping down to us step by step. As soon as it reached the huge masses amongst which we were painfully toiling, some of them would begin to jump about like hailstones in a shower, and our position would become really dangerous. The Chamouni guides, in fact, declared it to be dangerous already, and warned us not to speak, for fear of bringing some of the nicely-poised ice-masses down on our heads. On my translating this well-meant piece of advice to Lauener, he immediately selected the most dangerous looking pinnacle in sight, and mounting to the top of it sent forth a series of screams, loud enough, I should have thought, to bring down the top of the Mönch. They failed, however, to dislodge any *séracs*, and Lauener, going to the front, called to us to follow him. By this time we were all glad to follow any one who was confident enough to lead. Turning to our right, we crossed the glacier in a direction parallel to the deep crevasses, and therefore unobstructed by any serious obstacles, till we found ourselves immediately beneath the great cliffs of the Mönch. Our prospects changed at once. A great fold in the glacier produces a kind of diagonal pathway, stretching upwards from the point where we stood towards the rocks of the Eiger—not that it was exactly a carriage-road—but along the line which divides two different systems of crevasse, the glacier seemed to have been crushed into smaller fragments, producing, as it were, a kind of incipient macadamisation. The masses, instead of being divided by long regular trenches, were crumbled and jammed together so as to form a road, easy and pleasant enough by comparison with our former difficulties. Pressing rapidly up this rough path, we soon found ourselves in the very heart of the glacier, with a broken wilderness of ice on every side. We were in one of the grandest positions I have ever seen for observing the wonders of the ice-world; but those wonders were not all of an encouraging nature. For, looking up to the snow-fields now close above us, an obstacle appeared which made us think that all our previous labours had been in vain. From side to side of the glacier a vast *chevaux de frise* of blue ice-pinnacles struck up through the white layers of *névé* formed by the first plunge of the glacier down its waterfall of ice. Some of them rose in fantastic shapes—huge blocks balanced on narrow footstalks, and only waiting for the first touch of the sun to fall in ruins down the slope below. Others rose like church spires, or like square towers, defended by trenches of unfathomable depths. Once beyond this barrier we should be safe upon the highest plateau of the glacier at the foot of the last snow-slope. But it was obviously necessary to turn them by some judicious strategical movement. One plan was to climb the lower rocks of the Eiger; but, after a moment's hesitation, we fortunately followed Lauener towards the other side of the glacier, where a small gap between the *séracs* and the lower slopes of the Mönch seemed to be the entrance to a ravine that might lead us upwards. Such it turned out to be. Instead of the rough footing in which we had hitherto been unwillingly restricted, we found ourselves ascending a narrow gorge, with the giant cliffs of the Mönch on our right, and the toppling ice-pinnacles on our left. A beautifully even surface of snow, scarcely marked by a single crevasse, lay beneath our feet. We pressed rapidly up this strange little pathway, as it wound steeply upwards between the rocks and the ice, expecting at every moment to see it thin out, or break off at some impassable crevasse. It was, I presume, formed by the sliding of avalanches from the slopes of the Mönch. At any rate, to our delight, it led us gradually round the barrier of *séracs*, till in a few minutes we found ourselves on the highest plateau of the glacier, the crevasses fairly beaten, and a level plain of snow stretching from our feet to the last snow-slope.

"We were now standing on the edge of a small level plateau. One, and only one, gigantic crevasse of really surpassing beauty stretched right across it. This was, we guessed, some 300 feet deep, and its sides passed gradually into the lovely blues and greens of semi-transparent ice, whilst long rows and clusters of huge icicles imitated (as Lauener remarked) the carvings and ecclesiastical furniture of some great cathedral.

"To reach our pass, we had the choice either of at once attacking the long steep slopes which led directly to the shoulder of the Mönch, or of first climbing the gentle slope near the Eiger, and then forcing our way along the backbone of the ridge. We resolved to try the last plan first.

"Accordingly, after a hasty breakfast at 9.30, we started across our little snow-plain and commenced the ascent. After a short climb of no great difficulty, merely pausing to chip a few steps out of the hard crust of snow, we successively stepped safely on to the top of the ridge. As each of my predecessors did so, I observed that he first looked along the arête, then down the cliffs before him, and then turned with a very blank expression of face to his neighbour. From our feet the bare cliffs sank down, covered with loose rocks, but too steep to hold more than patches of snow, and presenting right dangerous climbing for many hundred feet towards the Grindelwald glaciers. The arête offered a prospect not much better: a long ridge of snow, sharp as the blade of a knife, was playfully alternated with great rocky teeth, striking up through their icy covering, like the edge of a saw. We held a council standing, and considered the following propositions:—First, Lauener coolly proposed, and nobody seconded, a descent of the precipices towards

Grindelwald. This proposition produced a subdued shudder from the travellers and a volley of unreportable language from the Chamouni guides. It was liable, amongst other things, to the trifling objection that it would take us just the way we did not want to go. The Chamouni men now proposed that we should follow the arête. This was disposed of by Lauener's objection that it would take at least six hours. We should have had to cut steps down the slope and up again round each of the rocky teeth I have mentioned; and I believe that this calculation of time was very probably correct. Finally, we unanimously resolved upon the only course open to us—to descend once more into our little valley, and thence to cut our way straight up the long slopes to the shoulder of the Mönch.

"Considerably disappointed at this unexpected check, we retired to the foot of the slopes, feeling that we had no time to lose, but still hoping that a couple of hours more might see us at the top of the pass. It was just eleven as we crossed a small bergschrund and began the ascent. Lauener led the way to cut the steps, followed by the two other guides, who deepened and polished them up. Just as we started, I remarked a kind of bright tract drawn down the ice in front of us, apparently by the frozen remains of some small rivulet which had been trickling down it. I guessed it would take some fifty steps and half-an-hour's work to reach it. We cut about fifty steps, however, in the first half-hour, and were not a quarter of the way to my mark; and as even when there we should not be half-way to the top, matters began to look serious. The ice was very hard, and it was necessary, as Lauener observed, to cut steps in it as big as soup-tureens, for the result of a slip would in all probability have been that the rest of our lives would have been spent in sliding down a snow-slope, and that that employment would not have lasted long enough to become at all monotonous. Time slipped by, and I gradually became weary of a sound to which at first I always listened with pleasure—the chipping of the axe, and the hiss of the fragments as they skip down the long incline below us. Moreover, the sun was very hot, and reflected with oppressive power from the bright and polished surface of the ice. I could see that a certain flask was circulating with great steadiness amongst the guides, and the work of cutting the steps seemed to be extremely severe. I was counting the 250th step, when we at last reached the little line I had been so long watching, and it even then required a glance back at the long line of steps behind to convince me that we had in fact made any progress. The action of resting one's whole weight on one leg for about a minute, and then slowly transferring it to the other, becomes wearisome when protracted for hours. Still the excitement and interest made the time pass quickly. I was in constant suspense lest Lauener should pronounce for a retreat, which would have been not merely humiliating, but not improbably dangerous, amidst the crumbling *séracs* in the afternoon sun. I listened with some amusement to the low moanings of little Charlet, who was apparently bewailing his position to Croz, and being heartless chaffed in return. One or two measurements with a clinometer of Mathews' gave inclinations of 51° or 52°, and the slope was perhaps occasionally a little more.

A VERY STEEP ICE SLOPE.

HARD SNOW IN THE EARLY MORNING ON THE TOP OF A GLACIER PASS NEARLY 12,000 FEET ABOVE SEA.

"At last, as I was counting the 580th step, we reached a little patch of rock, and felt ourselves once more on solid ground, with no small satisfaction. Not that the ground was specially solid. It was a small crumbling patch of rock, and every stone we dislodged went bounding rapidly down the side of the slope, diminishing in apparent size till it disappeared in the bergschrund, hundreds of feet below. However, each of us managed to find some nook in which he could stow himself away, whilst the Chamouni men took their turn in front, and cut steps straight upwards to the top of the slope. By this means they kept along a kind of rocky rib, of which our patch was the lowest point, and we thus could occasionally get a footstep on rock instead of ice. Once on the top of the slope, we could see no obstacle intervening between us and the point over which our pass must lie.

"Meanwhile we meditated on our position. It was already four o'clock. After twelve hours' unceasing labour, we were still a long way on the wrong side of the pass. We were clinging to a ledge in the mighty snow-wall which sank sheer down below us and rose steeply above our heads. Beneath our feet the whole plain of Switzerland lay with a faint purple haze drawn over it like a veil, a few green sparkles just pointing out the Lake of Thun. Nearer, and apparently almost immediately below us, lay the Wengern Alp, and the little inn we had left twelve hours before, whilst we could just see the back of the labyrinth of crevasses where we had wandered so long. Through a telescope I could even distinguish people standing about the inn, who no doubt were contemplating our motions. As we rested, the Chamouni guides had cut a staircase up the slope, and we prepared to follow. It was harder work than before, for the whole slope was now covered with a kind of granular snow, and resembled a huge pile of hailstones. The hailstones poured into every footstep as it was cut, and had to be cleared out with hands and feet before we could get even a slippery foothold. As we crept cautiously up this treacherous staircase, I could not help reflecting on the lively bounds with which the stones and fragments of ice had gone spinning from our last halting place down to the yawning bergschrund below. We succeeded, however, in avoiding their example, and a staircase of about one hundred steps brought us to the top of the ridge, but at a point still at some distance from the pass. It was necessary to turn along the arête towards the Mönch. We were preparing to do this by keeping on the snow-ridge, when Lauener, jumping down about 6 feet on the side opposite to that by which we had ascended, lighted upon a little ledge of rock, and called to us to follow. He assured us that it was granite, and that therefore there was no danger of slipping. It was caused by the sun having melted the snow on the southern side of the ridge, so that it no longer quite covered the inclined plane of rock upon which it rested. It was narrow and treacherous enough in appearance at first; soon, however, it grew broader, and, compared with our ice-climb, afforded capital footing. The precipice beneath us thinned out as the Viescher Glacier rose towards our pass, and at last we found ourselves at the edge of a little mound of snow, through which a few plunging steps brought us, just at six o'clock, to the long-desired shoulder of the Mönch.

"I cannot describe the pleasure with which we stepped at last on to the little saddle of snow, and felt that we had won the victory."

CHAPTER XVIII

THE AIGUILLE DU DRU

Few mountains have been the object of such repeated attempts by experienced climbers to reach their summits, as was the rocky pinnacle of the Aiguille du Dru, at Chamonix. While the name of Whymper will always be associated with the Matterhorn, so will that of Clinton Dent be with the Aiguille du Dru, and the accounts given by him in his delightful little work, *Above the Snow Line*, of his sixteen unavailing scrambles on the peak, followed by the stirring description of how at last he got up it, are amongst the romances of mountaineering.

I have space for only a few extracts describing Mr Dent's early attempts, which even the non-climber would find very entertaining to read about in the work from which I quote. The Chamonix people, annoyed that foreign guides should monopolise the peak, threw cold water on the idea of ascending it, and were ready, if they got a chance, to deny that it had been ascended. An honourable exception to the attitude adopted by these gentry, was, however, furnished by that splendid guide, Edouard Cupelin, who always asserted that the peak was climbable, and into whose big mind no trace of jealousy was ever known to enter.

Very witty are some of the accounts of Mr Dent's earlier starts for the Aiguille du Dru. On one occasion, starting in the small hours of the morning from Chamonix, he reached the Montanvert at 3.30 A.M. "The landlord at once appeared in full costume," he writes; "indeed I observed that during the summer it was impossible to tell from his attire whether he had risen immediately from bed or no. Our friend had cultivated to great perfection the art of half sleeping during his waking hours—that is, during such time as he might be called upon to provide entertainment for man and beast. Now, at the Montanvert, during the tourists' season, this period extended over the whole twenty-four hours. It was necessary, therefore, in order that he might enjoy a proper physiological period of rest, for him to remain in a dozing state—a sort of æstival hybernation—for the whole time, which in fact he did; or else he was by nature a very dull person, and had actually a very restricted stock of ideas.

"The sight of a tourist with an ice-axe led by a kind of reflex process to the landlord's unburdening his mind with his usual remarks. Like other natives of the valley he had but two ideas of 'extraordinary' expeditions. 'Monsieur is going to the Jardin?' he remarked. 'No, monsieur isn't.' 'Then, beyond a doubt, monsieur will cross the Col du Géant?' he said, playing his trump card. 'No, monsieur will not.' 'Pardon—where does monsieur expect to go?' 'On the present occasion we go to try the Aiguille du Dru.' The landlord smiled in an aggravating manner. 'Does monsieur think he will get up?' 'Time will show.' 'Ah!' The landlord, who had a chronic cold in the head, searched for his pocket-handkerchief, but not finding it, modified the necessary sniff into one of derision." On this day the party did not get up, nor did they gain the summit a little later when they made another attempt. They then had with them a porter who gave occasion for an excellent bit of character-sketching. "He was," says Mr Dent, "as silent as an oyster, though a strong and skilful climber, and like an oyster when its youth is passed, he was continually on the gape." They mounted higher and higher, and began at last to think that success awaited them. "Old Franz chattered away to himself, as was his wont when matters went well, and on looking back on one occasion I perceived the strange phenomenon of a smile illuminating the porter's features. However, this worthy spoke no words of satisfaction, but pulled ever at his empty pipe.

"By dint of wriggling over a smooth sloping stone slab, we had got into a steep rock gully which promised to lead us to a good height. Burgener, assisted by much pushing and prodding from below, and aided on his own part by much snorting and some strong language, had managed to climb on to a great overhanging boulder that cut off the view from the rest of the party below. As he disappeared from sight we watched the paying out of the rope with as much anxiety as a fisherman eyes his vanishing line when the salmon runs. Presently the rope ceased to move, and we waited for a few moments in suspense. We felt that the critical moment of the expedition had arrived, and the fact that our own view was exceedingly limited, made us all the more anxious to hear the verdict. 'How does it look?' we called out. The answer came back in *patois*, a bad sign in such emergencies. For a minute or two an animated conversation was kept up; then we decided to take another opinion, and accordingly hoisted up our second guides. The chatter was redoubled. 'What does it look like?' we shouted again. 'Not possible from where we are,' was the melancholy answer, and in a tone that crushed at once all our previous elation. I could not find words at the moment to express my disappointment; but the porter could, and gallantly he came to the rescue. He opened his mouth for the first time and spoke, and he said very loud indeed that it was 'verdammt.' Precisely: that is just what it was."

ON A VERY STEEP, SMOOTH SLAB OF ROCK.

NEGOTIATING STEEP PASSAGES OF ROCK.

It was not till 1878 that Mr Dent was able to return to Chamonix. He had now one fixed determination with regard to the Dru:—either he would get to the top or prove that the ascent was impossible.

His first few attempts that season were frustrated by bad weather, and so persistently did the rain continue to fall that for a couple of weeks no high ascents could be thought of. During this time, Mr Maund, who had been with Mr Dent on many of his attempts, was obliged to return to England.

"On a mountain such as we knew the Aiguille du Dru to be, it would not have been wise to make any attempt with a party of more than four. No doubt three —that is, an amateur with two guides—would have been better still, but I had, during the enforced inaction through which we had been passing, become so convinced of ultimate success, that I was anxious to find a companion to share it. Fortunately, J. Walker Hartley, a highly skilful and practised mountaineer, was at Chamouni, and it required but little persuasion to induce him to join our party. Seizing an opportunity one August day, when the rain had stopped for a short while, we decided to try once more, or, at any rate, to see what effects the climatic phases through which we had been passing had produced on the Aiguille. With Alexander Burgener and Andreas Maurer still as guides, we ascended once again the slopes by the side of the Charpoua Glacier, and succeeded in discovering a still more eligible site for a bivouac than on our previous attempts. A little before four the next morning we extracted each other from our respective sleeping bags, and made our way rapidly up the glacier. The snow still lay thick everywhere on the rocks, which were fearfully cold, and glazed with thin layers of slippery ice; but our purpose was very serious that day, and we were not to be deterred by anything short of unwarrantable risk. We intended the climb to be merely one of exploration, but were resolved to make it as thorough as possible, and with the best results. From the middle of the slope leading up to the ridge the guides went on alone, while we stayed to inspect and work out bit by bit the best routes over such parts of the mountain as lay within view. In an hour or two Burgener and Maurer came back to us, and the former invited me to go on with him back to the point from which he had just descended. His invitation was couched in gloomy terms, but there was a twinkle at the same time in his eye which it was easy to interpret—*ce n'est que l'œil qui rit*. We started off, and climbed without the rope up the way which was now so familiar, but which on this occasion, in consequence of the glazed condition of the rocks, was as difficult as it could well be; but for a growing conviction that the upper crags were not so bad as they looked, we should scarcely have persevered. 'Wait a little,' said Burgener, 'I will show you something presently.' We reached at last a great knob of rock close below the ridge, and for a long time sat a little distance apart silently staring at the precipices of the upper peak. I asked Burgener what it might be that he had to show me. He pointed to a little crack some way off, and begged that I would study it, and then fell again to gazing at it very hard himself. Though we scarcely knew it at the time this was the turning point of our year's climbing. Up to that moment I had only felt doubts as to the inaccessibility of the mountain. Now a certain feeling of confident elation began to creep over me. The fact is, that we gradually worked ourselves up into the right mental condition, and the aspect of a mountain varies marvellously according to the beholder's frame of mind. These same crags had been by each of us independently, at one time or another, deliberately pronounced impossible. They were in no better condition that day than usual, in fact, in much worse order than we had often seen them before. Yet, notwithstanding that good judges had ridiculed the idea of finding a way up the precipitous wall, the prospect looked different that day as turn by turn we screwed our determination up to the sticking point. Here and there we could clearly trace short bits of practicable rock ledges along which a man might walk, or over which at any rate he might transport himself, while cracks and irregularities seemed to develop as we looked. Gradually, uniting and communicating passages appeared to form. Faster and faster did our thoughts travel, and at last we rose and turned to each other. The same train of ideas had independently been passing through our minds. Burgener's face flushed, his eyes brightened, and he struck a great blow with his axe as we exclaimed almost together, 'It must, and it shall be done!'

"The rest of the day was devoted to bringing down the long ladder, which had previously been deposited close below the summit of the ridge, to a point much lower and nearer to the main peak. This ladder had not hitherto been of the slightest assistance on the rocks, and had, indeed, proved a source of constant anxiety and worry, for it was ever prone to precipitate its lumbering form headlong down the slope. We had, it is true, used it occasionally on the glacier to bridge over the crevasses, and had saved some time thereby. Still, we were loth to discard its aid altogether, and accordingly devoted much time and no little exertion to hauling it about and fixing it in a place of security. It was late in the evening before we had made all our preparations for the next assault and turned to the descent, which proved to be exceedingly difficult on this occasion. The snow had become very soft during the day; the late hour and the melting above caused the stones to fall so freely down the gully that we gave up that line of descent and made our way over the face. Often, in travelling down, we were buried up to the waist in soft snow overlying rock slabs, of which we knew no more than that they were very smooth and inclined at a highly inconvenient angle. It was imperative for one only to move at a time, and the perpetual roping and unroping was most wearisome. In one place it was necessary to pay out 150 feet of rope between one position of comparative security and the one next below it, till the individual who was thus lowered looked like a bait at the end of a deep sea-line. One step and the snow would crunch up in a wholesome manner and yield firm support. The next, and the leg plunged in as far as it could reach, while the submerged climber would, literally, struggle in vain to collect himself. Of course those above, to whom the duty of paying out the rope was entrusted, would seize the occasion to jerk as violently at the cord as a cabman does at his horse's mouth when he has misguided the animal round a corner. Now another step, and a layer of snow not more than a foot deep would slide off with a gentle hiss, exposing bare, black ice beneath, or treacherous loose stones. Nor were our difficulties at an end when we reached the foot of the rocks, for the head of the glacier had fallen away from the main mass of the mountain, even as an ill-constructed bow-window occasionally dissociates itself from the façade of a jerry-built villa, and some very complicated manœuvring was necessary in order to reach the snow slopes. It was not till late in the evening that we reached Chamouni; but it would have mattered nothing to us even had we been benighted, for we had seen all that we had wanted to see, and I would have staked my existence now on the possibility of ascending the peak. But the moment was not yet at hand, and our fortress held out against surrender to the very last by calling in its old allies, sou'-westerly winds and rainy weather. The whirligig of time had not yet revolved so as to bring us in our revenge.

"Perhaps the monotonous repetition of failures on the peak influences my recollection of what took place subsequently to the expedition last mentioned. Perhaps (as I sometimes think even now) an intense desire to accomplish our ambition ripened into a realisation of actual occurrences which really were only efforts of imagination. This much I know, that when on 7th September we sat once more round a blazing wood fire at the familiar bivouac gazing pensively at the crackling fuel, it seemed hard to persuade one's self that so much had taken place since our last attempt. Leaning back against the rock and closing the eyes for a moment it seemed but a dream, whose reality could be disproved by an effort of the will, that we had gone to Zermatt in a storm and hurried back again in a drizzle on hearing that some other climbers were intent on our peak; that we had left Chamouni in rain and tried, for the seventeenth time, in a tempest; that matters had seemed so utterly hopeless, seeing that the season was far advanced and the days but short, as to induce me to return to England, leaving minute directions that if the snow should chance to melt and the weather to mend I might be summoned back at once; that after eight-and-forty hours of sojourn in the fogs of my native land an intimation had come by telegraph of glad tidings; that I had posted off straightway by *grande vitesse* back to Chamouni; that I had arrived there at four in the morning."

Once more the party mounted the now familiar slopes above their bivouac, and somehow on this occasion they all felt that something definite would come of the expedition, even if they did not on that occasion actually reach the top.

I give the remainder of the account in Mr Dent's own words:

"Now, personal considerations had to a great extent to be lost sight of in the desire to make the most of the day, and the result was that Hartley must have had a very bad time of it. Unfortunately, perhaps for him, he was by far the lightest member of the party; accordingly we argued that he was far less likely to break the rickety old ladder than we were. Again, as the lightest weight, he was most conveniently lowered down first over awkward places when they occurred.

"In the times which are spoken of as old, and which have also, for some not very definable reason, the prefix good, if you wanted your chimneys swept you did not employ an individual now dignified by the title of a Ramoneur, but you adopted the simpler plan of calling in a master sweep. This person would come attended by a satellite, who wore the outward form of a boy and was gifted with certain special physical attributes. Especially was it necessary that the boy should be of such a size and shape as to fit nicely to the chimney, not so loosely on the one hand as to have any difficulty in ascending by means of his knees and elbows, nor so tightly on the other as to run any peril of being wedged in. The boy was then inserted into the chimney and did all the work, while the master remained below or sat expectant on the roof to encourage, to preside over, and subsequently to profit by, his apprentice's exertions. We adopted much the same principle. Hartley, as the lightest, was cast for the *rôle* of the *jeune premier*, or boy, while Burgener and I on physical grounds alone filled the part, however unworthily, of the master sweep. As a play not infrequently owes its success to one actor so did our *jeune premier*, sometimes very literally, pull us through on the present occasion. Gallantly indeed did he fulfil his duty. Whether climbing up a ladder slightly out of the perpendicular, leaning against nothing in particular and with overhanging rocks above; whether let down by a rope tied round his waist, so that he dangled like the sign of the 'Golden Fleece' outside a haberdasher's shop, or hauled up smooth slabs of rock with his raiment in an untidy heap around his neck; in each and all of these exercises he was equally at home, and would be let down or would come up smiling. One place gave us great difficulty. An excessively steep wall of rock presented itself and seemed to bar the way to a higher level. A narrow crack ran some little way up the face, but above the rock was slightly overhanging, and the water trickling from some higher point had led to the formation of a huge bunch of gigantic icicles, which hung down from above. It was necessary to get past these, but impossible to cut them away, as they would have fallen on us below. Burgener climbed a little way up the face, planted his back against it, and held on to the ladder in front of him, while I did the same just below: by this means we kept the ladder almost perpendicular, but feared to press the highest rung heavily against the icicles above lest we should break them off. We now invited Hartley to mount up. For the first few steps it was easy enough; but the leverage was more and more against us as he climbed higher, seeing that he could not touch the rock, and the strain on our arms below was very severe. However, he got safely to the top and disappeared from view. The performance was a brilliant one, but, fortunately, had not to be repeated; as on a subsequent occasion, by a deviation of about 15 or 20 feet, we climbed to the same spot in a few minutes with perfect ease and without using any ladder at all. On this occasion, however, we must have spent fully an hour while Hartley performed his feats, which were not unworthy of a Japanese acrobat. Every few feet of the mountain at this part gave us difficulty, and it was curious to notice how, on this the first occasion of travelling over the rock face, we often selected the wrong route in points of detail. We ascended from 20 to 25 feet, then surveyed right and left, up and down, before going any further. The minutes slipped by fast, but I have no doubt now that if we had had time we might have ascended to the final arête on this occasion. We had often to retrace our steps, and whenever we did so found some slightly different line by which time could have been saved. Though the way was always difficult nothing was impossible, and when the word at last was given, owing to the failing light, to descend, we had every reason to be satisfied with the result of the day's exploration. There seemed to be little doubt that we had traversed the most difficult part of the mountain, and, indeed, we found on a later occasion, with one or two notable exceptions, that such was the case.

"However, at the time we did not think that, even if it were possible, it would be at all advisable to make our next attempt without a second guide. A telegram had been sent to Kaspar Maurer, instructing him to join us at the bivouac with all possible expedition. The excitement was thus kept up to the very last, for we knew not whether the message might have reached him, and the days of fine weather were precious.

"It was late in the evening when we reached again the head of the glacier, and the point where we had left the feeble creature who had started with us as a second guide. On beholding us once more he wept copiously, but whether his tears were those of gratitude for release from the cramped position in which he had spent his entire day, or of joy at seeing us safe again, or whether they were the natural overflow of an imbecile intellect stirred by any emotion whatever, it were hard to say; at any rate he wept, and then fell to a description of some interesting details concerning the proper mode of bringing up infants, and the duties of parents towards their children; the most important of which, in his estimation, was that the father of a family should run no risk whatever on a mountain. Reaching our bivouac, we looked anxiously down over the glacier for any signs of Kaspar Maurer. Two or three parties were seen crawling homewards towards the Montanvert over the ice-fields, but no signs of our guide were visible. As the shades of night, however, were falling, we were able indistinctly to see in the far-off distance a little black dot skipping over the Mer de Glace with great activity. Most eagerly did we watch the apparition, and when finally it headed in our direction, and all doubt was removed as to the personality, we felt that our constant ill-luck was at last on the eve of changing. However, it was not till two days later that we left Chamouni once more for the nineteenth, and, as it proved, for the last time to try the peak.

"On 11th September we sat on the rocks a few feet above the camping-place. Never before had we been so confident of success. The next day's climb was no longer to be one of exploration. We were to start as early as the light would permit, and we were to go up and always up, if necessary till the light should fail. Possibly we might have succeeded long before if we had had the same amount of determination to do so that we were possessed with on this occasion. We had made up our minds to succeed, and felt as if all our previous attempts had been but a sort of training for this special occasion. We had gone so far as to instruct our friends below to look out for us on the summit between twelve and two the next day. We had even gone to the length of bringing a stick wherewith to make a flagstaff on the top. Still one, and that a very familiar source of disquietude, harassed us as our eyes turned anxiously to the west. A single huge band of cloud hung heavily right across the sky, and looked like a harbinger of evil, for it was of a livid colour above, and tinged with a deep crimson red below. My companion was despondent at the prospect it suggested, and the guides tapped their teeth with their forefingers when they looked in that direction; but it was suggested by a more sanguine person that its form and very watery look suggested a Band of Hope. An insinuating smell of savoury soup was wafted up gently from below—

'Stealing and giving odour.'

We took courage; then descended to the tent, and took sustenance.

"There was no difficulty experienced in making an early start the next day, and the moment the grey light allowed us to see our way we set off. On such occasions, when the mind is strung up to a high pitch of excitement, odd and trivial little details and incidents fix themselves indelibly on the memory. I can recall as distinctly now, as if it had only happened a moment ago, the exact tone of voice in which Burgener, on looking out of the tent, announced that the weather would do. Burgener and Kaspar Maurer were now our guides, for our old enemy with the family ties had been paid off and sent away with a flea in his ear—an almost unnecessary adjunct, as anyone who had slept in the same tent with him could testify. Notwithstanding that Maurer was far from well, and, rather weak, we mounted rapidly at first, for the way was by this time familiar enough, and we all meant business.

"Our position now was this. By our exploration on the last occasion we had ascertained that it was possible to ascend to a great height on the main mass of the mountain. From the slope of the rocks, and from the shape of the mountain, we felt sure that the final crest would be easy enough. We had then to find a way still up the face, from the point where we had turned back on our last attempt, to some point on the final ridge of the mountain. The rocks on this part we had never been able to examine very closely, for it is necessary to cross well over to the south-eastern face while ascending from the ridge between the Aiguille du Dru and the Aiguille Verte. A great projecting buttress of rock, some two or three hundred feet in height, cuts off the view of that part of the mountain over which we now hoped to make our way. By turning up straight behind this buttress, we hoped to hit off and reach the final crest just above the point where it merges into the precipitous north-eastern wall visible from the Chapeau. This part of the mountain can only be seen from the very head of the Glacier de la Charpoua just under the mass of the Aiguille Verte. But this point of view is too far off for accurate observations, and the strip of mountain was practically, therefore, a *terra incognita* to us.

"We followed the gully running up from the head of the glacier towards the ridge above mentioned, keeping well to the left. Before long it was necessary to cross the gully on to the main peak. To make the topography clearer a somewhat prosaic and domestic simile may be employed. The Aiguille du Dru and the Aiguille Verte are connected by a long sharp ridge, towards which we were now climbing; and this ridge is let in, as it were, into the south-eastern side of the Aiguille du Dru, much as a comb may be stuck into the middle of a hairbrush, the latter article representing the main peak. Here we employed the ladder which had been placed in the right position the day previously. Right glad were we to see the rickety old structure, which had now spent four years on the mountain, and was much the worse for it. It creaked and groaned dismally under our weight, and ran sharp splinters into us at all points of contact, but yet there was a certain companionship about the old ladder, and we seemed almost to regret that it was not destined to share more in our prospective success. A few steps on and we came to a rough cleft some five-and-twenty feet in depth, which had to be descended. A double rope was fastened to a projecting crag, and we swung ourselves down as if we were barrels of split peas going into a ship's hold; then to the ascent again, and the excitement waxed stronger as we drew nearer to the doubtful part of the mountain. Still, we did not anticipate insuperable obstacles; for I think we were possessed with a determination to succeed, which is a sensation often spoken of as a presentiment of success. A short climb up an easy broken gully, and of a sudden we seemed to be brought to a stand still. A little ledge at our feet curled round a projecting crag on the left. 'What are we to do now?' said Burgener, but with a smile on his face that left no doubt as to the answer. He lay flat down on the ledge and wriggled round the projection, disappearing suddenly from view, as if the rock had swallowed him up. A shout proclaimed that his expectations had not been deceived, and we were bidden to follow; and follow we did, sticking to the flat face of the rock with all our power, and progressing like the skates down the glass sides of an aquarium tank. When the last man joined us we found ourselves all huddled together on a very little ledge indeed, while an overhanging rock above compelled us to assume the anomalous attitude enforced on the occupant of a little-ease dungeon. What next? An eager look up solved part of the doubt. 'There is the way,' said Burgener, leaning back to get a view. 'Oh, indeed,' we answered. No doubt there was a way, and we were glad to hear that it was possible to get up it. The attractions of the route consisted of a narrow flat gully plastered up with ice, exceeding straight and steep, and crowned at the top with a pendulous mass of enormous icicles. The gully resembled a half-open book standing up on end. Enthusiasts in rock-climbing who have ascended the Riffelhorn from the Gorner Glacier side will have met with a similar gully, but, as a rule, free from ice, which, in the present instance, constituted the chief difficulty. The ice, filling up the receding angle from top to bottom, rendered it impossible to find handhold on the rocks, and it was exceedingly difficult to cut steps in such a place, for the slabs of ice were prone to break away entire. However, the guides said they could get up, and asked us to keep out of the way of chance fragments of ice which might fall down as they ascended. So we tucked ourselves away on one side, and they fell to as difficult a business as could well be imagined. The rope was discarded, and slowly they worked up, their backs and elbows against one sloping wall, their feet against the other. But the angle was too wide to give security to this position, the more especially that with shortened axes they were compelled to hack out enough of the ice to reveal the rock below. In such places the ice is but loosely adherent, being raised up from the face much as pie-crust dissociates itself from the fruit beneath under the influence of the oven. Strike lightly with the axe, and a hollow sound is yielded without much impression on the ice; strike hard, and the whole mass breaks away. But the latter method is the right one to adopt, though it necessitates very hard work. No steps are really reliable when cut in ice of this description.

"The masses of ice, coming down harder and harder as they ascended without intermission, showed how they were working, and the only consolation we had during a time that we felt to be critical, was that the guides were not likely to expend so much labour unless they thought that some good result would come of it. Suddenly there came a sharp shout and cry; then a crash as a great slab of ice, falling from above, was dashed into pieces at our feet and leaped into the air; then a brief pause, and we knew not what would happen next. Either the gully had been ascended or the guides had been pounded, and failure here might be failure altogether. It is true that Hartley and I had urged the guides to find a way some little distance to the right of the line on which they were now working; but they had reported that, though easy below, the route we had pointed out was impossible above.[10] A faint scratching noise close above us, as of a mouse perambulating behind a wainscot. We look up. It is the end of a rope. We seize it, and our pull from below is answered by a triumphant yell from above as the line is drawn taut. Fastening the end around my waist, I started forth. The gully was a scene of ruin, and I could hardly have believed that two axes in so short a time could have dealt so much destruction. Nowhere were the guides visible, and in another moment there was a curious sense of solitariness as I battled with the obstacles, aided in no small degree by the rope. The top of the gully was blocked up by a great cube of rock, dripping still where the icicles had just been broken off. The situation appeared to me to demand deliberation, though it was not accorded. 'Come on,' said voices from above. 'Up you go,' said a voice from below. I leaned as far back as I could, and felt about for a handhold. There was none. Everything seemed smooth. Then right, then left; still none. So I smiled feebly to myself, and called out, 'Wait a minute.' This was, of course, taken as an invitation to pull vigorously, and, struggling and kicking like a spider irritated by tobacco smoke, I topped the rock, and lent a hand on the rope for Hartley to follow. Then we learnt that a great mass of ice had broken away under Maurer's feet while they were in the gully, and that he must have fallen had not Burgener pinned him to the rock with one hand. From the number of times that this escape was described to us during that day and the next, I am inclined to think that it was rather a near thing. At the time, and often since, I have questioned myself as to whether we could have got up this passage without the rope let down from above. I think either of us could have done it in time with a companion. It was necessary for two to be in the gully at the same time, to assist each other. It was necessary, also, to discard the rope, which in such a place could only be a source of danger. But no amateur should have tried the passage on that occasion without confidence in his own powers, and without absolute knowledge of the limit of his own powers. If the gully had been free from ice it would have been much easier.

"'The worst is over now,' said Burgener. I was glad to hear it, but looking upwards, had my doubts. The higher we went the bigger the rocks seemed to be. Still there was a way, and it was not so very unlike what I had, times out of mind, pictured to myself in imagination. Another tough scramble, and we stood on a comparatively extensive ledge. With elation we observed that we had now climbed more than half of the only part of the mountain of the nature of which we were uncertain. A few steps on and Burgener grasped me suddenly by the arm. 'Do you see the great red rock up yonder?' he whispered, hoarse with excitement— 'in ten minutes we shall be there and on the arête, and then——' Nothing could stop us now; but a feverish anxiety to see what lay beyond, to look on the final slope which we knew must be easy, impelled us on, and we worked harder than ever to overcome the last few obstacles. The ten minutes expanded into something like thirty before we really reached the rock. Of a sudden the mountain seemed to change its form. For hours we had been climbing the hard, dry rocks. Now these appeared suddenly to vanish from under our feet, and once again our eyes fell on snow which lay thick, half hiding, half revealing, the final slope of the ridge. A glance along it showed that we had not misjudged. Even the cautious Maurer admitted that, as far as we could see, all appeared promising. And now, with the prize almost within our grasp, a strange desire to halt and hang back came on. Burgener tapped the rock with his axe, and we seemed somehow to regret that the way in front of us must prove comparatively easy. Our foe had almost yielded, and it appeared something like cruelty to administer the final *coup de grâce*. We could already anticipate the half-sad feeling with which we should reach the top itself. It needed but little to make the feeling give way. Some one cried 'Forward,' and instantly we were all in our places again, and the leader's axe crashed through the layers of snow into the hard blue ice beneath. A dozen steps, and then a short bit of rock scramble; then more steps along the south side of the ridge, followed by more rock, and the ridge beyond, which had been hidden for a minute or two, stretched out before us again as we topped the first eminence. Better and better it looked as we went on. 'See there,' cried Burgener suddenly, 'the actual top!'

"There was no possibility of mistaking the two huge stones we had so often looked at from below. They seemed, in the excitement of the moment, misty and blurred for a brief space, but grew clear again as I passed my hand over my eyes, and seemed to swallow something. A few feet below the pinnacles and on the left was one of those strange arches formed by a great transverse boulder, so common near the summits of these aiguilles, and through the hole we could see blue sky. Nothing could lay beyond, and, still better, nothing could be above. On again, while we could scarcely stand still in the great steps the leader set his teeth to hack out. Then there came a short troublesome bit of snow scramble, where the heaped-up cornice had fallen back from the final rock. There we paused for a moment, for the summit was but a few feet from us, and Hartley, who was ahead, courteously allowed me to unrope and go on first. In a few seconds I clutched at the last broken rocks, and hauled myself up on to the sloping summit. There for a moment I stood alone gazing down on Chamouni. The holiday dream of five years was accomplished; the Aiguille du Dru was climbed. Where in the wide world will you find a sport able to yield pleasure like this?"

CHAPTER XIX

THE MOST FAMOUS MOUNTAIN IN THE ALPS—THE CONQUEST OF THE MATTERHORN

The story of the Matterhorn must always be one of unique attraction. Like a good play, it resumes and concentrates in itself the incidents of a prolonged struggle—the conquest of the Alps. The strange mountain stood forth as a Goliath in front of the Alpine host, and when it found its conqueror there was a general feeling that the subjugation of the High Alps by human effort was decided, a feeling which has been amply justified by events. The contest itself was an eventful one. It was marked by a race between eager rivals, and the final victory was marred by the most terrible of Alpine accidents.

Mr and Mrs Seiler and three of their Daughters. Zermatt, 1890.

Going leisurely to Zermatt with a Mule for the luggage in the olden days.

"As a writer, Mr Whymper has proved himself equal to his subject. His serious, emphatic style, his concentration on his object, take hold of his readers and make them follow his campaigns with as much interest as if some great stake depended on the result. No one can fail to remark the contrast between the many unsuccessful attacks which preceded the fall of the Matterhorn, and the frequency with which it is now climbed by amateurs, some of whom it would be courtesy to call indifferent climbers. The moral element has, of course, much to do with this. But allowance must also be made for the fact that the Breil ridge, which looks the easiest, is still the most difficult, and in its unbechained state was far the most difficult. The terrible appearance of the Zermatt and Zmutt ridges long deterred climbers, yet both have now yielded to the first serious attack."

These words, taken from a review of Mr Whymper's *Ascent of the Matterhorn*, occur in vol. ix. on page 441 of *The Alpine Journal*. They are as true now as on the day when they appeared, but could the writer have known the future history of the great peak, and the appalling vengeance it called down over and over again on "amateurs" and the guides who, themselves unfit, tempted their ignorant charges to go blindly to their deaths, one feels he would have stood aghast at the contemplation of the tragedies to be enacted on the blood-stained precipices of that hoary peak.

THE CONQUEST OF THE MATTERHORN

When one remembers all the facilities for climbing which are found at present in every Alpine centre, the experienced guides who may be had, the comfortable huts which obviate the need for a bivouac out of doors, the knowledge of the art of mountaineering which is available if any desire to acquire it, one marvels more and more at the undaunted persistence displayed by the pioneers of present-day mountaineering in their struggle with the immense difficulties which beset them on every side.

When, in 1861, Mr Whymper made his first attempt on the Matterhorn, the first problem he had to solve was that of obtaining a skilful guide. Michael Croz of Chamonix believed the ascent to be impossible. Bennen thought the same. Jean Antoine Carrel was dictatorial and unreasonable in his demands, though convinced that the summit could be gained. Peter Taugwalder asked 200 francs whether the top was reached or not. "Almer asked, with more point than politeness, 'Why don't you try to go up a mountain which *can* be ascended?'"

In 1862 Mr Whymper, who had three times during the previous summer tried to get up the mountain, returned to Breuil on the Italian side, and thence made five plucky attempts, sometimes with Carrel, and once alone, to go to the highest point it was possible to reach. On the occasion of his solitary climb, Mr Whymper had set out from Breuil to see if his tent, left on a ledge of the mountain, was still, in spite of recent storms, safely in its place. He found all in good order, and tempted to linger by the lovely weather, time slipped away, and he at last decided to sleep that night in the tent, which contained ample provisions for several days. The next morning Mr Whymper could not resist an attempt to explore the route towards the summit, and eventually he managed to reach a considerable height, much above that attained by any of his predecessors. Exulting in the hope of entire success in the near future, he returned to the tent. "My exultation was a little premature," he writes, and goes on to describe what befell him on the way down. I give the thrilling account of his adventure in his own words:—

"About 5 P.M. I left the tent again, and thought myself as good as at Breuil. The friendly rope and claw had done good service, and had smoothened all the difficulties. I lowered myself through the chimney, however, by making a fixture of the rope, which I then cut off, and left behind, as there was enough and to spare. My axe had proved a great nuisance in coming down, and I left it in the tent. It was not attached to the bâton, but was a separate affair—an old navy boarding-axe. While cutting up the different snow-beds on the ascent, the bâton trailed behind fastened to the rope; and, when climbing, the axe was carried behind, run through the rope tied round my waist, and was sufficiently out of the way; but in descending when coming down face outwards (as is always best where it is possible), the head or the handle of the weapon caught frequently against the rocks, and several times nearly upset me. So, out of laziness if you will, it was left in the tent. I paid dearly for the imprudence.

"The Col du Lion was passed, and fifty yards more would have placed me on the 'Great Staircase,' down which one can run. But, on arriving at an angle of the cliffs of the Tête du Lion, while skirting the upper edge of the snow which abuts against them, I found that the heat of the two past days had nearly obliterated the steps which had been cut when coming up. The rocks happened to be impracticable just at this corner, and it was necessary to make the steps afresh. The snow was too hard to beat or tread down, and at the angle it was all but ice; half a dozen steps only were required, and then the ledges could be followed again. So I held to the rock with my right hand, and prodded at the snow with the point of my stick until a good step was made, and then, leaning round the angle, did the same for the other side. So far well, but in attempting to pass the corner (to the present moment I cannot tell how it happened), I slipped and fell.

"The slope was steep on which this took place, and was at the top of a gully that led down through two subordinate buttresses towards the Glacier du Lion —which was just seen a thousand feet below. The gully narrowed and narrowed, until there was a mere thread of snow lying between two walls of rock, which came to an abrupt termination at the top of a precipice that intervened between it and the glacier. Imagine a funnel cut in half through its length, placed at an angle of 45° with its point below, and its concave side uppermost, and you will have a fair idea of the place.

"The knapsack brought my head down first, and I pitched into some rocks about a dozen feet below; they caught something and tumbled me off the edge, head over heels, into the gully; the bâton was dashed from my hands, and I whirled downwards in a series of bounds, each longer than the last; now over ice, now into rocks; striking my head four or five times, each time with increased force. The last bound sent me spinning through the air, in a leap of 50 or 60 feet, from one side of the gully to the other, and I struck the rocks, luckily, with the whole of my left side. They caught my clothes for a moment, and I fell back on to the snow with motion arrested. My head, fortunately, came the right side up, and a few frantic catches brought me to a halt in the neck of the gully, and on the verge of the precipice. Bâton, hat, and veil skimmed by and disappeared, and the crash of the rocks—which I had started —as they fell on to the glacier, told how narrow had been the escape from utter destruction. As it was, I fell nearly 200 feet in seven or eight bounds. Ten feet more would have taken me in one gigantic leap of 800 feet on to the glacier below.

"The situation was sufficiently serious. The rocks could not be let go for a moment, and the blood was spirting out of more than twenty cuts. The most serious ones were in the head, and I vainly tried to close them with one hand, whilst holding on with the other. It was useless; the blood jerked out in blinding jets at each pulsation. At last, in a moment of inspiration, I kicked out a big lump of snow, and stuck it as a plaster on my head. The idea was a happy one, and the flow of blood diminished. Then, scrambling up, I got, not a moment too soon, to a place of safety, and fainted away. The sun was setting when consciousness returned, and it was pitch dark before the Great Staircase was descended; but, by a combination of luck and care, the whole 4900 feet of descent to Breuil was accomplished without a slip, or once missing the way. I slunk past the cabin of the cowherds, who were talking and laughing inside, utterly ashamed of the state to which I had been brought by my imbecility, and entered the inn stealthily, wishing to escape to my room unnoticed. But Favre met me in the passage, demanded 'Who is it?' screamed with fright when he got a light, and aroused the household. Two dozen heads then held solemn council over mine, with more talk than action. The natives were unanimous in recommending that hot wine mixed with salt should be rubbed into the cuts; I protested, but they insisted. It was all the doctoring they received. Whether their rapid healing was to be attributed to that simple remedy or to a good state of health is a question. They closed up remarkably quickly, and in a few days I was able to move again."

In 1863 Mr Whymper once more returned to the attack, but still without success. In 1864 he was unable to visit the neighbourhood of the Matterhorn, but in 1865 he made his eighth and last attempt on the Breuil, or Italian side.

The time had now come when Mr Whymper became convinced that it was an error to think the Italian side the easier. It certainly looked far less steep than the north, or Zermatt side, but on mountains quality counts for far more than quantity; and though the ledges above Breuil might sometimes be broader than those on the Swiss side, and the general slope of the mountain appear at a distance to be gentler, yet the rock had an unpleasant outward dip, giving sloping, precarious hold for hand or foot, and every now and then there were abrupt walls of rock which it was hardly possible to ascend, and out of the question to descend without fixing ropes or chains.

THE GUIDES' WALL, ZERMATT.

Now the Swiss side of the great peak differs greatly from its Italian face. The slope is really less steep, and the ledges, if narrow, slope inward, and are good to step on or grasp. Mr Whymper had noticed that large patches of snow lay on the mountain all the summer, which they could not do if the north face was a precipice. He determined, therefore, to make his next attempt on that side. He had, in 1865, intended to climb with Michel Croz, but some misunderstanding had arisen, and Croz, believing that he was free, had engaged himself to another traveller. His letter, "the last one he wrote to me," says Mr Whymper, is "an interesting souvenir of a brave and upright man." The following is an extract from it:

"enfin, Monsieur, je regrette beaucoup d'être engagè avec votre compatriote et de ne pouvoir vous accompagner dans vos conquetes mais dès qu'on a donnè sa parole on doit la tenir et être homme.

"Ainsi, prenez patience pour cette campagne et esperons que plus tard nous nous retrouverons.

"En attendant recevez les humbles salutations de votre tout devoué.

"Croz Michel-Auguste."

By an extraordinary series of chances, however, when Mr Whymper reached Zermatt, whom should he see sitting on the guides' wall but Croz! His employer had been taken ill, and had returned home, and the great guide was immediately engaged by the Rev. Charles Hudson for an attempt on the Matterhorn! Mr Whymper had been joined by Lord Francis Douglas and the Taugwalders, father and son, and thus two parties were about to start for the Matterhorn at the same hour next day. This was thought inadvisable, and eventually they joined forces and decided to set out the following morning together. Mr Hudson had a young man travelling with him, by name Mr Hadow, and when Mr Whymper enquired if he were sufficiently experienced to take part in the expedition, Mr Hudson replied in the affirmative, though the fact that Mr Hadow had recently made a very rapid ascent of Mont Blanc really proved nothing. Here was the weakest spot in the whole business, the presence of a youth, untried on difficult peaks, on a climb which might involve work of a most unusual kind. Further, we should now-a-days consider the party both far too large and wrongly constituted, consisting as it did of four amateurs, two good guides, and a porter.

On 13th July, 1865, at 5.30 A.M., they started from Zermatt in cloudless weather. They took things leisurely that day, for they only intended going a short distance above the base of the peak, and by 12 o'clock they had found a good position for the tent at about 11,000 feet above sea. The guides went on some way to explore, and on their return about 3 P.M. declared that they had not found a single difficulty, and that success was assured.

THE ZERMATT SIDE OF THE MATTERHORN.

The route now usually followed has been kindly marked by Sir W. Martin Conway. The first party, on reaching the snow patch near the top, bore somewhat to their right to avoid a nearly vertical wall of rock, where now hangs a chain.

From a Photograph by the late W. F. Donkin.

RISING MISTS.

The following morning, as soon as it was light enough to start, they set out, and without trouble they mounted the formidable-looking north face, and approached the steep bit of rock which it is now customary to ascend straight up by means of a fixed chain. But they were obliged to avoid it by diverging to their right on to the slope overhanging the Zermatt side of the mountain. This involved somewhat difficult climbing, made especially awkward by the thin film of ice which at places overlay the rocks. "It was a place over which any fair mountaineer might pass in safety," writes Mr Whymper, and neither here nor anywhere else on the peak did Mr Hudson require the slightest help. With Mr Hadow, however, the case was different, his inexperience necessitating continual assistance.

Before long this solitary difficulty was passed, and, turning a rather awkward corner, the party saw with delight that only 200 feet or so of easy snow separated them from the top!

Yet even then it was not certain that they had not been beaten, for a few days before another party, led by Jean Antoine Carrel, had started from Breuil, and might have reached the much-desired summit before them.

The slope eased off more and more, and at last Mr Whymper and Croz, casting off the rope, ran a neck and neck race to the top. Hurrah! not a footstep could be seen, and the snow at both ends of the ridge was absolutely untrampled.

"Where were the men?" Mr Whymper wondered, and peering over the cliffs of the Italian side he saw them as dots far down. They were 1250 feet below, yet they heard the cries of the successful party on the top, and knew that victory was not for them. Still a measure of success awaited them too, for the next day the bold Carrel, with J. B. Bich, in his turn reached the summit by the far more difficult route on the side of his native valley. Carrel was the one man who had always believed that the Matterhorn could be climbed, and one can well understand Mr Whymper's generous wish that he could have shared in the first ascent.

One short hour was spent on the summit. Then began the ever-eventful descent.

The climbers commenced to go down the difficult piece in the following order: Croz first, Hadow next, then Mr Hudson, after him Lord Francis Douglas, then old Taugwalder, and lastly Mr Whymper, who gives an account of what happened almost immediately after in the following words:

"A few minutes later a sharp-eyed lad ran into the Monte Rosa Hotel to Seiler, saying that he had seen an avalanche falling from the summit of the Matterhorn on to the Matterhorngletscher. The boy was reproved for telling idle stories; he was right, nevertheless, and this was what he saw:

"Michel Croz had laid aside his axe, and in order to give Mr Hadow greater security, was absolutely taking hold of his legs, and putting his feet, one by one, into their proper positions.[11] So far as I know, no one was actually descending. I cannot speak with certainty, because the two leading men were partially hidden from my sight by an intervening mass of rock, but it is my belief, from the movements of their shoulders, that Croz, having done as I have said, was in the act of turning round, to go down a step or two himself; at this moment Mr Hadow slipped, fell against him, and knocked him over. I heard one startled exclamation from Croz, then saw him and Mr Hadow flying downwards. In another moment Hudson was dragged from his steps, and Lord Francis Douglas immediately after him.[12] All this was the work of a moment. Immediately we heard Croz's exclamation old Peter and I planted ourselves as firmly as the rocks would permit;[13] the rope was taut between us, and the jerk came on us both as on one man. We held, but the rope broke midway between Taugwalder and Lord Francis Douglas. For a few seconds we saw our unfortunate companions sliding downwards on their backs, and spreading out their hands, endeavouring to save themselves. They passed from our sight uninjured, disappeared one by one, and fell from precipice to precipice on to the Matterhorngletscher below, a distance of nearly 4000 feet in height. From the moment the rope broke it was impossible to help them. So perished our comrades!"

A BITTERLY COLD DAY, 13,000 FEET ABOVE SEA.

The Matterhorn from the Zmutt side.

The dotted line shows the course which the unfortunate party probably took in their fatal fall.

A more terrible position than that of Mr Whymper and the Taugwalders it is difficult to imagine. The Englishman kept his head, however, though the two guides, absolutely paralysed with terror, lost all control over themselves, and for a long time could not be induced to move. At last old Peter changed his position, and soon the three stood close together. Mr Whymper then examined the broken rope, and found to his horror that it was the weakest of the three ropes, and had only been intended as a reserve to fix to rocks and leave behind. How it came to have been used will always remain a mystery, but that it broke and was not cut there is no doubt. Taugwalder's neighbours at Zermatt persisted in asserting that he severed the rope. "In regard to this infamous charge," writes Mr Whymper, "I say that he *could* not do so at the moment of the slip, and that the end of the rope in my possession shows that he did not do so beforehand."

At 6 P.M., after a terribly trying descent, during any moment of which the Taugwalders, still completely unnerved, might have slipped and carried the whole party to destruction, they arrived on "the ridge descending towards Zermatt, and all peril was over." But it was still a long way to the valley, and an hour after nightfall the climbers were obliged to seek a resting-place, and upon a slab barely large enough to hold the three they spent six miserable hours. At daybreak they started again, and descended rapidly to Zermatt.

"Seiler met me at the door. 'What is the matter?' 'The Taugwalders and I have returned.' He did not need more, and burst into tears."

At 2 A.M. on Sunday the 16th, Mr Whymper and two other Englishmen, with a number of Chamonix and Oberland guides, set out to discover the bodies. The Zermatt men, threatened with excommunication by their priests if they failed to attend early Mass were unable to accompany them, and to some of them this was a severe trial. By 8.30 they reached the plateau at the top of the glacier, and came within sight of the spot where their companions must be. "As we saw one weather-beaten man after another raise the telescope, turn deadly pale, and pass it on without a word to the next, we knew that all hope was gone."

They drew near, and found the bodies of Croz, Hadow and Hudson close together, but of Lord Francis Douglas they could see nothing, though a pair of gloves, a belt and a boot belonging to him were found. The boots of all the victims were off, and lying on the snow close by. This frequently happens when persons have fallen a long distance down rocks.

Eventually the remains were brought down to Zermatt, a sad and dangerous task.

So ends the story of the conquest of the Matterhorn. Its future history is marred by many a tragedy, of which perhaps none are more pathetic, or were more wholly unnecessary, than what is known as the Borckhardt accident.

CHAPTER XX

SOME TRAGEDIES ON THE MATTERHORN

By the summer of 1886 it had become common for totally inexperienced persons with incompetent guides (for no first-rate guide would undertake such a task) to make the ascent of the Matterhorn. In fine settled weather they contrived to get safely up and down the mountain. But like all high peaks the Matterhorn is subject to sudden atmospheric changes, and a high wind or falling snow will in an hour or less change the whole character of the work and make the descent one of extreme difficulty even for experienced mountaineers. Practically unused to Alpine climbing, thinly clothed, and accompanied by young guides of third-rate ability, what wonder is it that when caught in a storm, a member of the party, whose expedition is described below, perished?

JOST, FOR MANY YEARS PORTER OF THE MONTE ROSA HOTEL, ZERMATT.

The editor of *The Alpine Journal* writes: "On the morning of 17th August last four parties of travellers left the lower hut on the mountain and attained the summit. One of them, that of Mr Mercer, reached Zermatt the same night. The three others were much delayed by a sudden storm which came on during the descent. Two Dutch gentlemen, led by Moser and Peter Taugwald, regained the lower hut at an advanced hour of the night; but Monsieur A. de Falkner and his son (with J. P. and Daniel Maquignaz, and Angelo Ferrari, of Pinzolo), and Messrs John Davies and Frederick Charles Borckhardt (with Fridolin Kronig and Peter Aufdemblatten), were forced to spend the night out; the latter party, indeed, spent part of the next day (18th August) out as well, and Mr Borckhardt unfortunately succumbed to the exposure in the afternoon. He was the youngest son of the late vicar of Lydden, and forty-eight years of age. Neither he nor Mr Davies was a member of the Alpine Club."

The Pall Mall Gazette published on 24th August the account given by Mr Davies to an interviewer. It is as follows, and the inexperience of the climbers is made clear in every line:-

"We left Zermatt about 2 o'clock on Monday afternoon in capital spirits. The weather was lovely, and everything promised a favourable ascent. We had two guides whose names were on the official list, whose references were satisfactory, and who were twice over recommended to us by Herr Seiler, whose advice we sought before we engaged them, and who gave them excellent credentials. We placed ourselves in their hands, as is the rule in such cases, ordered the provisions and wine which they declared to be necessary, and made ready for the ascent. I had lived among hills from my boyhood. I had some experience of mountaineering in the Pyrenees, where I ascended the highest and other peaks. In the Engadine I have also done some climbing; and last week, together with Mr Borckhardt, who was one of my oldest friends, I made the ascent of the Titlis, and made other excursions among the hills. Mr Borckhardt was slightly my senior, but as a walker he was quite equal to me in endurance. When we arrived at Zermatt last Saturday we found that parties were going up the Matterhorn on Monday. We knew that ladies had made the ascent, and youths; and the mountain besides had been climbed by friends of ours whose physical strength, to say the least, was not superior to ours. It was a regular thing to go up the Matterhorn, and we accordingly determined to make the ascent.

"We started next morning at half-past two or three. We were the third party to leave the cabin, but, making good speed over the first stage of the ascent, we reached the second when the others were breakfasting there, and then resumed the climb. Mr Mercer, with his party, followed by the Dutch party, started shortly before us. We met them about a quarter-past eight returning from the top. They said that they had been there half an hour, and that there was no view. We passed them, followed by the Italians, and reached the summit about a quarter to nine. The ascent, though toilsome, had not exhausted us in the least. Both Mr Borckhardt and myself were quite fresh, although we had made the summit before the Italians, who started together with us from the second hut. Had the weather remained favourable, we could have made the descent with ease.[14]

"Even while we were on the summit I felt hail begin to fall, and before we were five minutes on our way down it was hailing heavily. It was a fine hail, and inches of it fell in a very short time, and the track was obliterated. We pressed steadily downwards, followed by the Italians, nor did it occur to me at that time that there was any danger. We got past the ropes and chains safely, and reached the snowy slope on the shoulder. At this point we were leading. But as the Italians had three guides, and we only two, we changed places, so that their third guide could lead. They climbed down the slope, cutting steps for their feet in the ice. We trod closely after the Italians, but the snow and hail filled up the holes so rapidly, that, in order to make a safe descent, our guides had to recut the steps. This took much time—as much as two hours I should say—and every hour the snow was getting deeper. At last we got down the snow-slope on to the steep rocks below. The Italians were still in front of us, and we all kept on steadily descending. We were still in good spirits, nor did we feel any doubt that we should reach the bottom. Our first alarm was occasioned by the Italians losing their way. They found their progress barred by precipitous rocks, and their guides came back to ours to consult as to the road. Our guides insisted that the path lay down the side of a steep couloir. Their guides demurred; but after going down some ten feet, they cried out that our guides were right, and they went on—we followed. By this time it was getting dark. The hail continued increasing. We began to get alarmed. It seemed impossible to make our way to the cabin that night. We had turned to the right after leaving the couloir, crossed some slippery rocks, and after a short descent turned to the left and came to the edge of the precipice where Mosely fell, where there was some very slight shelter afforded by an overhanging rock, and there we prepared to pass the night, seeing that all further progress was hopeless. We were covered with ice. The night was dark. The air was filled with hail. We were too cold to eat. The Italians were about an hour below us on the mountain side. We could hear their voices and exchanged shouts. Excepting them, we were thousands of feet above any other human being. I found that while Borckhardt had emptied his brandy-flask, mine was full. I gave him half of mine. That lasted us through the night.

We did not try the wine till the morning, and then we found that it was frozen solid.

"Never have I had a more awful experience than that desolate night on the Matterhorn. We were chilled to the bone, and too exhausted to stand. The wind rose, and each gust drove the hail into our faces, cutting us like a knife. Our guides did everything that man could do to save us. Aufdemblatten did his best to make us believe that there was no danger. 'Only keep yourselves warm; keep moving; and we shall go down all right to-morrow, when the sun rises.' 'It is of no use,' I replied; 'we shall die here!' They chafed our limbs, and did their best to make us stand up; but it was in vain. I felt angry at their interference. Why could they not leave us alone to die? I remember striking wildly but feebly at my guide as he insisted on rubbing me. Every movement gave me such agony, I was racked with pain, especially in my back and loins —pain so intense as to make me cry out. The guides had fastened the rope round the rock to hold on by, while they jumped to keep up the circulation of the blood. They brought us to it, and made us jump twice or thrice. Move we could not; we lay back prostrate on the snow and ice, while the guides varied their jumping by rubbing our limbs and endeavouring to make us move our arms and legs. They were getting feebler and feebler. Borckhardt and I, as soon as we were fully convinced that death was imminent for us, did our best to persuade our guides to leave us where we lay and make their way down the hill. They were married men with families. To save us was impossible; they might at least save themselves. We begged them to consider their wives and children and to go. This was at the beginning of the night. They refused. They would rather die with us, they said; they would remain and do their best.

Hoar Frost in the Alps.

Hoar Frost in the Alps.

"Borckhardt and I talked a little as men might do who are at the point of death. He bore without complaining pain that made me cry out from time to time. We both left directions with the guides that we were to be buried at Zermatt. Borckhardt spoke of his friends and his family affairs, facing his death with manly resignation and composure. As the night wore on I became weaker and weaker. I could not even make the effort necessary to flick the snow off my companion's face. By degrees the guides began to lose hope. The cold was so intense, we crouched together for warmth. They lay beside us to try and impart some heat. It was in vain. 'We shall die!' 'We are lost!' 'Yes,' said Aufdemblatten, 'very likely we shall.' He was so weak, poor fellow, he could hardly keep his feet; but still he tried to keep me moving. It was a relief not to be touched. I longed for death, but death would not come.

"Towards half-past two on Wednesday morning—so we reckoned, for all our watches had stopped with the cold—the snow ceased, and the air became clear. It had been snowing or hailing without intermission for eighteen hours. It was very dark below, but above all was clear, although the wind still blew.

When the sun rose, we saw just a gleam of light. Then a dark cloud came from the hollow below, and our hopes went out. 'Oh, if only the sun would come out!' we said to each other, I do not know how many times. But it did not, and instead of the sun came the snow once more. Towards seven, as near as I can make it, a desperate attempt was made to get us to walk. The guides took Borckhardt, and between them propped him on his feet and made him stagger on a few steps. They failed to keep him moving more than a step or two. The moment they let go he dropped. They repeated the same with me. Neither could I stand. I remember four distinct times they drove us forward, only to see us drop helpless after each step. It was evidently no use. Borckhardt had joined again with me in repeatedly urging the guides to leave us and to save themselves. They had refused, and continued to do all that their failing strength allowed to protect us from the bitter cold. As the morning wore on, my friend, who during the night had been much more composed and tranquil than I, began to grow perceptibly weaker. We were quite resigned to die, and had, in fact, lost all hope. We had been on the mountain from about 3 A.M. on Tuesday to 1 P.M. on Wednesday—thirty-four hours in all. Eighteen of these were spent in a blinding snowstorm, and we had hardly tasted food since we left the summit at nine on the Tuesday morning. At length (about one) we heard shouts far down the mountain. The guides said they probably proceeded from a search party sent out to save us. I again urged the guides to go down by themselves to meet the searchers, and to hurry them up. This they refused to do unless I accompanied them. Borckhardt was at this time too much exhausted to stand upright, and was lying in a helpless condition. The guides, although completely worn out, wished to attempt the descent with me, and they considered that by so doing we should be able to indicate to the searchers the precise spot where my friend lay, and to hasten their efforts to reach him with stimulants. Since early morning the snow had ceased falling. We began the descent, and at first I required much assistance from the guides, but by degrees became better able to move, and the hope of soon procuring help from the approaching party for my poor friend sustained us. After a most laborious descent of about an hour and a half, we reached the first members of the rescue party, and directed them to where Borckhardt lay, requesting them to proceed there with all haste, and, after giving him stimulants, to bring him down to the lower hut in whatever condition they found him. We went on to the hut to await his arrival, meeting on the way Mr King, of the English Alpine Club, with his guides, who were hurrying up with warm clothing. A few hours later we heard the terrible news that the relief party had found him dead."

A letter to *The Times*, written by Mr (now Sir Henry Seymour) King comments as follows on this deplorable accident. It is endorsed by all the members of the Alpine Club then at Zermatt. After describing the circumstances of the ascent, the writer continues: "Instead of staying all together, as more experienced guides would have done, and keeping Mr Borckhardt warm and awake until help came, they determined at about 1 P.M. to leave him alone on the mountain. According to their account, the snow had ceased and the sun had begun to shine when they left him. At that moment a relief party was not far off, as the guides must have known. They heard the shouts of the relief party soon after leaving Mr Borckhardt, and there was, as far as I can see, no pressing reason for their departure. They reached the lower hut at about 5 P.M., and at about the same time a rescue party from Zermatt, which had met them descending, reached Mr Borckhardt, and found him dead, stiff, and quite cold, and partly covered with freshly-fallen snow. No doubt he had succumbed to drowsiness soon after he was left.

"The moral of this most lamentable event is plain. The Matterhorn is not a mountain to be played with; it is not a peak which men ought to attempt until they have had some experience of climbing. Above all, it is not a peak which should ever be attempted except with thoroughly competent guides. In a snowstorm no member of a party should ever be left behind and alone. He will almost certainly fall into a sleep, from which it is notorious that he will never awake. If he will not walk, he must be carried. If he sits down, he must be made to get up. Guides have to do this not unfrequently. A stronger and more experienced party would undoubtedly have reached Zermatt without misfortune. In fact, one party which was on the mountain on the same day did reach Zermatt in good time."

It is fitting that this short, and necessarily incomplete, account of the conquest of the Matterhorn, and events occurring subsequently on it, should conclude with the recital of a magnificent act of heroism performed by Jean-Antoine Carrel, whose name, more than that of any other guide, is associated with the history of the peak. No more striking instance of the devotion of a guide to his employers could be chosen to bring these true tales of the hills to an appropriate end.

I take the account from *Scrambles Among the Alps.*

"When telegrams came in, at the beginning of September 1890, stating that Jean-Antoine Carrel had died from fatigue on the south side of the Matterhorn, those who knew the man scarcely credited the report. It was not likely that this tough and hardy mountaineer would die from fatigue anywhere, still less that he would succumb upon 'his own mountain.' But it was true. Jean-Antoine perished from the combined effects of cold, hunger, and fatigue, upon his own side of his own mountain, almost within sight of his own home. He started on the 23rd of August from Breuil, with an Italian gentleman and Charles Gorret (brother of the Abbé Gorret), with the intention of crossing the Matterhorn in one day. The weather at the time of their departure was the very best, and it changed in the course of the day to the very worst. They were shut up in the *cabane* at the foot of the Great Tower during the 24th, with scarcely any food, and on the 25th retreated to Breuil. Although Jean-Antoine (upon whom, as leading guide, the chief labour and responsibility naturally devolved) ultimately succeeded in getting his party safely off the mountain, he himself was so overcome by fatigue, cold, and want of food, that he died on the spot."

Jean-Antoine Carrel entered his sixty-second year in January 1901,[15] and was in the field throughout the summer. On 21st August, having just returned from an ascent of Mont Blanc, he was engaged at Courmayeur by Signor Leone Sinigaglia, of Turin, for an ascent of the Matterhorn. He proceeded to the Val Tournanche, and on the 23rd set out with him and Charles Gorret, for the last time, to ascend his own mountain by his own route. A long and clear account of what happened was communicated by Signor Sinigaglia to the Italian Alpine Club, and from this the following relation is condensed:

"We started for the Cervin at 2.15 A.M. on the 23rd, in splendid weather, with the intention of descending the same night to the hut at the Hörnli on the Swiss side. We proceeded pretty well, but the glaze of ice on the rocks near the Col du Lion retarded our march somewhat, and when we arrived at the hut at the foot of the Great Tower, prudence counselled the postponement of the ascent until the next day, for the sky was becoming overcast. We decided upon this, and stopped.

"Here I ought to mention that both I and Gorret noticed with uneasiness that Carrel showed signs of fatigue upon leaving the Col du Lion. I attributed this to temporary weakness. As soon as we reached the hut he lay down and slept profoundly for two hours, and awoke much restored. In the meantime the weather was rapidly changing. Storm clouds coming from the direction of Mont Blanc hung over the Dent d'Hérens, but we regarded them as transitory, and trusted to the north wind, which was still continuing to blow. Meanwhile, three of the Maquignazs and Edward Bich, whom we found at the hut, returned from looking after the ropes, started downwards for Breuil, at parting wishing us a happy ascent, and holding out hopes of a splendid day for the morrow.

"But, after their departure, the weather grew worse very rapidly; the wind changed, and towards evening there broke upon us a most violent hurricane of hail and snow, accompanied by frequent flashes of lightning. The air was so charged with electricity that for two consecutive hours in the night one could see in the hut as in broad daylight. The storm continued to rage all night, and the day and night following, continuously, with incredible violence. The temperature in the hut fell to 3 degrees.

"The situation was becoming somewhat alarming, for the provisions were getting low, and we had already begun to use the seats of the hut as firewood. The rocks were in an extremely bad state, and we were afraid that if we stopped longer, and the storm continued, we should be blocked up in the hut for several days. This being the state of affairs, it was decided among the guides that if the wind should abate we should descend on the following morning; and, as the wind did abate somewhat, on the morning of the 25th (the weather, however, still remaining very bad) it was unanimously settled to make a retreat.

"At 9 A.M. we left the hut. I will not speak of the difficulties and dangers in descending the *arête* to the Col du Lion, which we reached at 2.30 P.M. The ropes were half frozen, the rocks were covered with a glaze of ice, and fresh snow hid all points of support. Some spots were really as bad as could be, and I owe much to the prudence and coolness of the two guides that we got over them without mishap.

"At the Col du Lion, where we hoped the wind would moderate, a dreadful hurricane recommenced, and in crossing the snowy passages we were nearly *suffocated* by the wind and snow which attacked us on all sides.[16] Through the loss of a glove, Gorret, half an hour after leaving the hut, had already got a hand frost-bitten. The cold was terrible here. Every moment we had to remove the ice from our eyes, and it was with the utmost difficulty that we could speak so as to understand one another.

"Nevertheless, Carrel continued to direct the descent in a most admirable manner, with a coolness, ability, and energy above all praise. I was delighted to see the change, and Gorret assisted him splendidly. This part of the descent presented unexpected difficulties, and at several points great dangers, the more so because the *tourmente* prevented Carrel from being sure of the right direction, in spite of his consummate knowledge of the Matterhorn. At 11 P.M. (or thereabouts, it was impossible to look at our watches, as all our clothes were half frozen) we were still toiling down the rocks. The guides sometimes asked each other where they were; then we went forward again—to stop, indeed, would have been impossible. Carrel at last, by marvellous instinct, discovered the passage up which we had come, and in a sort of grotto we stopped a minute to take some brandy.

"While crossing some snow we saw Carrel slacken his pace, and then fall back two or three times to the ground. Gorret asked him what was the matter, and he said 'nothing,' but he went on with difficulty. Attributing this to fatigue through the excessive toil, Gorret put himself at the head of the caravan, and Carrel, after the change, seemed better, and walked well, though with more circumspection than usual. From this place a short and steep passage takes one down to the pastures, where there is safety. Gorret descended first, and I after him. We were nearly at the bottom when I felt the rope pulled. We stopped, awkwardly placed as we were, and cried out to Carrel several times to come down, but we received no answer. Alarmed, we went up a little way, and heard him say, in a faint voice, 'Come up and fetch me; I have no strength left.'

"We went up and found that he was lying with his stomach to the ground, holding on to a rock, in a semi-conscious state, and unable to get up or to move a step. With extreme difficulty we carried him to a safe place, and asked him what was the matter. His only answer was, 'I know no longer where I am.' His hands were getting colder and colder, his speech weaker and more broken, and his body more still. We did all we could for him, putting with great difficulty the rest of the cognac into his mouth. He said something, and appeared to revive, but this did not last long. We tried rubbing him with snow, and shaking him, and calling to him continually, but he could only answer with moans.

"We tried to lift him, but it was impossible—he was getting stiff. We stooped down, and asked in his ear if he wished to commend his soul to God. With a last effort he answered 'Yes,' and then fell on his back, dead, upon the snow.

"Such was the end of Jean-Antoine Carrel—a man who was possessed with a pure and genuine love of mountains; a man of originality and resource, courage and determination, who delighted in exploration. His special qualities marked him out as a fit person to take part in new enterprises, and I preferred him to all others as a companion and assistant upon my journey amongst the Great Andes of the Equator. Going to a new country, on a new continent, he encountered much that was strange and unforeseen; yet when he turned his face homewards he had the satisfaction of knowing that he left no failures behind him.[17] After parting at Guayaquil in 1880 we did not meet again. In his latter years, I am told, he showed signs of age, and from information which has been communicated to me it is clear that he had arrived at a time when it would have been prudent to retire—if he could have done so. It was not in his nature to spare himself, and he worked to the very last. The manner of his death strikes a chord in hearts he never knew. He recognised to the fullest extent the duties of his position, and in the closing act of his life set a brilliant example of fidelity and devotion. For it cannot be doubted that, enfeebled as he was, he could have saved himself had he given his attention to self-preservation. He took a nobler course; and, accepting his responsibility, devoted his whole soul to the welfare of his comrades, until, utterly exhausted, he fell staggering on the snow. He was already dying. Life was flickering, yet the brave spirit said 'It is *nothing*.' They placed him in the rear to ease his work. He was no longer able even to support himself; he dropped to the ground, and in a few minutes expired."[18]

CHAPTER XXI

THE WHOLE DUTY OF THE CLIMBER—ALPINE DISTRESS SIGNALS

I cannot bring this book to a more fitting end than by quoting the closing words of a famous article in *The Alpine Journal* by Mr C. E. Mathews entitled "The Alpine Obituary." It was written twenty years ago, but every season it becomes if possible more true. May all who go amongst the mountains lay it to heart!

"Mountaineering is extremely dangerous in the case of incapable, of imprudent, of thoughtless men. But I venture to state that of all the accidents in our sad obituary, there is hardly one which need have happened; there is hardly one which could not have been easily prevented by proper caution and proper care. Men get careless and too confident. This does not matter or the other does not matter. The fact is, that everything matters; precautions should be not only ample but excessive.

'The little more, and how much it is,

And the little less and what worlds away.'

"Mountaineering is not dangerous, provided that the climber knows his business and takes the necessary precautions—all within his own control—to make danger impossible. The prudent climber will recollect what he owes to his family and to his friends. He will also recollect that he owes something to the Alps, and will scorn to bring them into disrepute. He will not go on a glacier without a rope. He will not climb alone, or with a single companion. He will treat a great mountain with the respect it deserves, and not try to rush a dangerous peak with inadequate guiding power. He will turn his back steadfastly upon mist and storm. He will not go where avalanches are in the habit of falling after fresh snow, or wander about beneath an overhanging glacier in the heat of a summer afternoon. Above all, if he loves the mountains for their own sake, for the lessons they can teach and the happiness they can bring, he will do nothing that can discredit his manly pursuit or bring down the ridicule of the undiscerning upon the noblest pastime in the world."

ALPINE DISTRESS SIGNALS

No book on climbing should be issued without a reminder to its readers that tourists (who may need it even oftener than mountaineers) have a means ready to hand by which help can be signalled for if they are in difficulties. That in many cases a signal might not be seen is no reason for neglecting to learn and use the simple code given below and recommended by the Alpine Club. It has now been adopted by all societies of climbers.

The signal is the repetition of a sound, a wave of a flag, or a flash of a lantern *at regular intervals* at the rate of six signals per minute, followed by a pause of a minute, and then repeated every alternate minute. The reply is the same, except that three and not six signals are made in a minute. The regular minute's interval is essential to the clearness of the code.

[1]

Lightning Source UK Ltd.
Milton Keynes UK
UKHW010635240820
368739UK00001B/199